NEIL A...

Playing on
the Edge

Looking for Easy

PUFFIN BOOKS

Published by the Penguin Group
Penguin Books Ltd, 27 Wrights Lane, London W8 5TZ, England
Penguin Putnam Inc., 375 Hudson Street, New York, New York 10014, USA
Penguin Books Australia Ltd, Ringwood, Victoria, Australia
Penguin Books Canada Ltd, 10 Alcorn Avenue, Toronto, Ontario, Canada M4V 3B2
Penguin Books (NZ) Ltd, Private Bag 102902, NSMC, Auckland, New Zealand

On the World Wide Web at: www.penguin.com

Penguin Books Ltd, Registered Offices: Harmondsworth, Middlesex, England

First published 2000
2

Set in 11½ /14 Palatino

Made and printed in England by Clays Ltd, St Ives plc

British Library Cataloguing in Publication Data
A CIP catalogue record for this book is available from the British Library

ISBN 0–141–30750–1

CONTENTS

A Report into the State of Football in the UK, December 2063

Soccer is now the No 1 sport in both the US and China (knocking basketball off its lofty pedestal). Football can, at last, be said to have achieved total global domination. In London this year, the FA celebrates its second centenary.

One hundred years on from 'Wembley 1966', this country will host the World Cup final for only the second time in its history. But three decades of mergers, acquisitions and take-overs have seen the old familiar clubs of soccer's mother-nation melt away and vanish. With thirty months still to go before 'Wembley 2066', England's chances in the competition are already the subject of much speculation.

But what is the state of the game in this country?

There are currently just two leagues playing football in Britain.

The **British Premier League** (BPL): super-teams whose composite names reflect their soccer pedigree. For example:

Gunman Reds (Arsenal, Man United, Forest, Liverpool)

New Spurs United (Newcastle United, Tottenham Hotspur, Derby and Notts County)

Blue City Rangers (Manchester City, Glasgow Rangers, Chelsea, Everton)

The **Corporates League** (CL): newly-created

nation-less teams that bear the names of their owners, the *mega-multis*, the world's twenty biggest international companies.

Since the World Cup of 1966 the gap between rich and poor in this country has widened immeasurably. Watching football has become an expensive luxury pastime. In both leagues, clubs and their players are enormously wealthy. The ordinary supporter has, for a long time, only been able to watch matches via pay-per-view — at home (not a cheap option) or, more commonly, on the giant screens of the leisure palaces (large-scale premises licensed for drinking, gambling and screening games).

As a consequence, the underground Unaffiliated Football League (UFL) has mushroomed in popularity. The UFL is a national network of small clubs, playing at unlicensed, squatted and sometimes even makeshift venues, often with impromptu pitch-side betting. Illegal and prone to police raids, UFL games are skilful, rough-and-ready, high-drama affairs, popular with talent scouts. Though invariably local, they are reaching far wider audiences courtesy of the pirate channels.

But BPL and CL have immense power and influence. They control the FA. They are in league with IFFA. And they are rumoured to have government ministers in their pockets.

With the aid of *enhancers*, chemical stimulants that increase growth and performance, players are being brought into the professional game at an increasingly young age. Today's game is fast and skilful. But there can be no disputing the risks of permanent damage from injury, and these are greatest for boys who play before achieving full physical development.

In an attempt to stave off criticism the authorities (football and government) have recently published a list of 'Category P' enhancers. The enhancers on this list are deemed by the authorities to be safe and their use is permitted. As for the long-term side-effects of enhancers, Category P or otherwise, to date there is insufficient evidence available for assessment.

It's been a dismal century for the nation, on and off the pitch. Many say the rot set in way back in 1966 when, with that infamous disallowed goal of the final, England lost their grip on the World Cup. For both the national side and the domestic game it's been downhill ever since: chopped and changed, corrupted and priced out of reach.

Twenty-five World Cups later, England needs to rewrite its history. Will they, in three years' time, have players with the courage, brilliance, audacity and team spirit that are needed for this task? That remains to be seen.

Professor Arsene Ilyk
Department of Soccer Studies,
University of Sport

1
LEVEL PLAYING FIELD

The adverts ended.

'Don't forget, tonight on BBC Sport, *Goalarama*: coverage of the monster clash: Gunman Reds versus Blue City Rangers. No doubt about it – it's going to be a thrill-a-minute match. But twice the excitement when you watch it here, with us.

'Yes, once again, we'll be on the pitch with the players. Exclusive access to all player-to-player and manager-to-player communications. The BBC's unique epaulette micro-cameras bringing you player-point-of-view shots at all the critical moments, throughout the game. *Plus* press-of-a-button interactive action replay. *You* call the shots!

'There will, of course, be unrivalled commentary: the usual suspects down at Highbury, and big-name guests here in the studio, watching the game and sharing their views with us in our post-match analysis.

'It's going to be one stupendous night of football action. There's only one place to be: *Goalarama* ... on the BBC.'

Towering above Highbury Fields, the Gunman Reds' stadium gleamed in the sunlight.

Easy swerved, slipped past the first defender and accelerated inside the second. He glanced back. Heads jerking, arms and legs pumping, players thundered behind. No chance of support – his nearest teammate was way back. Any waiting around and the advantage would be lost.

'Go for it!'

'Gowaan, Easy – do the business!'

Had they been playing on a pitch, with lines and goal posts and everything, he'd be inside the penalty area by now. Closing fast from an angle, he skipped a high tackle, barged between the last two defenders and charged towards a pile of bags and jackets – the nearside post.

The keeper came out low, spreading wide his big gloved hands.

Easy changed tack, dancing the ball, searching for a way past. The keeper scowled. Easy dummied a lob. The keeper sprang, too late he saw the trap and tried to check his flight – Easy's ball, gently toe-poked, was through his legs and over the line.

'Naaaaah!'

'Yeeeees!'

Game over. Easy cartwheeled and ran towards the onlookers.

'Easy! Easy!' Trix, his younger sister and proudest, most loyal fan, proclaimed her delight. 'Way to go, bro!'

'Another hat trick.' Deena, his older sister, affected a yawn and turned to look away. 'Trix ...' She nudged her sister and pointed. 'That man over by the tree – have you noticed?'

Trix nodded. 'Every now and then he starts jabbering.' She tapped her skull. 'Must be bonkers.'

Deena chuckled and shook her head. 'I don't think so. I was watching him. He only really chatted when something clever was going down with the ball. I reckon he's wearing a discrete communicator. He's either recording his impressions, or reporting them to someone direct.'

Trix looked puzzled. 'Why would he want to do either?'

'You really are clueless, aren't you?' Deena tutted, raising her gaze heavenward. 'Because, stupid – he's part of a ring of evil blood-sucking fiends ...' Her voice deepened. '... with a taste for the flesh of young boys.'

'Eurgh!' Trix's face contorted, uncertain whether to be horrified or repulsed.

'They *devour* them!' Deena gave a blood-curdling laugh. 'Come on, Trix! You can't go on being gullible all your life. Surely, it's obvious?'

Trix shook her head.

'He's a talent scout from New Spurs United.' She frowned. 'Or Blue City Rangers maybe. Who knows? Perhaps one of the other big clubs thinks they can steal our home-grown talent.'

Trix pouted and grabbed her brother's hand. 'They can't have him!'

'Don't worry!' Easy laughed. 'No one's poaching me! Deena's winding you up. The guy's probably nuts and jabbering to himself like you said. Or maybe he's chatting to his wife on his communicator, telling her what time he'll be home for his tea.'

'Oh yeah …' Deena snorted derisively. '… he just happens to "chat" at all the moments someone makes a good pass, or a clever interception. And each time you've scored.'

Easy shrugged. 'Talent scouts aren't going to come round here. None of us'd even be tempted. We're all die-hard Reds.'

Trix threw her arms round her brother. 'Our next big star!'

'And don't you forget it!' Lifting her off her feet, Easy spun round.

'Watch the size of that head!' Deena scowled and folded her arms. 'If you're so *hot*, how come Dad hasn't got you signed up?'

Easy staggered, giddy. Deena always got sour round the question of his footballing talent. 'Dad's in a tricky position. You know how cautious and conscientious he is. He'd never risk anything that might be interpreted as favouritism. He knows how good I am – so what's the rush? I can't play pro till I'm fourteen.'

'But you can get on the training programme at thirteen. That's only a few months away.'

'Deena, come on! He doesn't need to sign me up. They sign up the talent they're worried might go elsewhere.'

'You think you're so good, don't you?'

Easy didn't think, he *knew*. He'd met some excellent players in the Youth League and Inter-Schools Cup, but only once had he come across someone who might have been his match. He'd never had the chance to find out if the freckle-faced boy could better him on the pitch, because he had been in an older age category and, in spite of his incredible skills, his team had been knocked out in the very first round. Of course, nation-wide there were bound to be others as good. But they were extremely rare, according to Dad.

Easy shrugged. 'With the right development over the next two or three years, I might become something ...' With the right development, Dad had told him, he had the potential to become *truly exceptional*. Those were Dad's words. And as chief talent scout for Gunman Reds, his dad ought to know.

'You know it's true.' Trix prodded her sister. 'Easy's special with a ball. Everyone says so. You're just jealous.'

'Yeah, right,' snapped Deena. 'Like it was always my dream to be a soccer star.'

Easy leaped, somersaulted backwards, and landed on his bed beside the football. *'Yeeees!'* He punched at the ceiling ... 'Yes!' ...tweaked up the volume on the remote ... 'Yes!' ...settled back to watch the replay. *'Yes!'*

'*Oh!* What a truly *unbelievable* goal! Without doubt, that fabulous touch – in what must surely be the final few seconds – has clinched this game for Gunman Reds. It's been a game of two halves: two formidable sides battling it out and – *yes!* – there goes the final whistle. The capacity crowd in this one-hundred-and-twenty-thousand-seater stadium are on their feet, cheering and applauding. Supporters from both clubs acknowledging the stupendous quality of play we've witnessed here this evening.'

The image on the screen cut from pitch to studio – Jim Dryden talking to camera. 'Now then ... our reporter down in the tunnel is Gary Numan and, in a minute, he's going to try to grab a word with a couple of the players. We'll be bringing you that just as soon as we can, in the meantime ... oh, hang on ... yep, I think we can go straight to Gary now ... Gary?'

The image cut to inside the tunnel, Gary Numan mike in hand. 'Hi there, Jim. I've managed to grab Ajax Morayne, scorer of what were arguably the two most spectacular goals on the park this evening.' The camera shot widened to include Ajax Morayne. 'Ajax ... eighteen years old, four years as a pro – three with Gunman Reds, you're clearly on good form at the moment. We've never seen you play better ...' Gary thrust the mike towards the striker's chin. ' ... have we?'

Ajax shrugged and wiped a dangling lock from his brow. 'Dunno, Gary. Hard for me to say, to be honest.' Traces of a continental mother-tongue underpinned the London accent. The sweat-drenched brow furrowed. He grinned. 'I think today probably tops everything!'

'That final shot, Ajax – quite remarkable. Want to hazard a guess at how fast it was?'

Ajax grinned wider. 'Pretty fast! No idea.' He looked sheepish. 'Did you guys clock it?'

'You bet!' Gary touched his earpiece. 'Sorry, didn't quite catch that ... one hundred and *eighty*?' He nodded. 'Yep, the boys in the monitor room are confirming as we speak, right now: one hundred and eighty kilometres an hour!'

'Nah! Serious?'

'Would we lie to you?'

Ajax shook his head. 'Incredible!'

Gary touched the earpiece again. 'And that, apparently, is a new world record! Congratulations!'

'Thanks ... thanks, Gary.'

'The icing on the cake.'

'Yeah, right. Fantastic game ... Hughesie, Bladerkopf, Leonardo, Ze ... all the lads really – just phenomenal!'

'And Rangers?'

'Outstanding, Gary. I wouldn't want to take anything away from them. They played magnificently. Shame for them the way it turned out, but as we all know only too well – football is a fickle game.'

'Indeed. Now, Ajax, I know you must be itching to get back with the lads, to celebrate today's victory *and* your new world record, but could you give us a quick comment on IFFA's latest ruling regarding performance-enhancers?'

'Sure ...' Ajax coughed to clear his throat. 'Football is changing so fast these days. Basically, the way I see it – with every major team getting hooked up to one of the big international pharmaceutical companies, something like this was bound to happen sooner or later, yeah? Everyone's been saying it: with so much laboratory power focused on the development of enhancers, IFFA's ability to test for them just couldn't keep pace.'

'Critics have called the new ruling a *climb down*.'

'OK – yeah.' Ajax nodded sagely. 'People are entitled to their opinions. Personally, I think the creation of the so-called Category P list was inevitable – the only sensible course to take under the circumstances.'

'A case of moving with the times?'

'Exactly that, Gary.'

'And how about yourself, Ajax? Do you have feelings on whether the use of enhancers detracts in any way from the quality of the performance?'

'What can I say ...' Ajax grinned and shrugged. 'You watched the match, Gary. I'd say definitely not!'

'Well ...' Gary chuckled. 'Listening to those fans out there, I'd have to say they one-hundred-per-cent agree with you!'

'Yeah. And at the end of the day, they are the ones that matter.'

'Indeed ...'

The screen went blank. Easy fumbled in the dark for the remote. The room lights came up, dimmed. '*Dad!* You gave me a fright!'

'Sorry ...' Todd Linker sighed and placed the remote on the duvet.

Easy waited, but his father said nothing. He seemed lost in thought. The silence made Easy uncomfortable. 'How long have you been standing there?'

'Came in on the final whistle.' His voice was flat, tired-sounding. He rubbed the back of his neck. 'You were pretty caught up in it.' His eyes flitted to the dead screen. 'Good result.'

'Totally brilliant!' Easy cracked his knuckles. 'Our eighth consecutive win away – we're on a roll.'

Todd nodded. 'It would've been nice to have been there together.' His face caught the light – it looked drawn. He frowned. 'Sorry. I hate it when we have to miss stuff because of work.'

'That's OK, Dad.' Easy smacked the duvet. 'I like watching from home – it's more relaxed. Besides ...' He jumped up, scooping the football into the air with his instep, up on to his head. '... it won't be long now before I'm *playing* those matches!'

'Yes ...' The eyebrows lifted wearily. '... not far off now.'

Easy tilted his head back, bouncing the ball in tightly controlled little pulses from his forehead. 'I can't wait.'

'I know ...' The frown returned. 'I know.'

Easy caught the ball and sat. His father's face struggled with a smile. Something was troubling him. He seemed almost ... sad. 'Everything all right, Dad?'

'How d'you mean?' The shadows beneath Todd's eyes looked like bruises in the low light.

'You seem sort of ... I don't know ... tired?'

Sighing, Todd reached an arm round Easy's shoulders. 'Do I look that bad? Things really must be getting to me.' Pulling his son close, he ruffled his hair.

Easy hugged back. His father's body heaved with another sigh.

'Bedtime,' said Todd. 'Things always look brighter after a good night's sleep.' He kissed Easy's cheek. 'Goodnight, son.'

Easy kissed his father back.

2

DARK SKIES

The red neon outline of a cannon burned into the darkening sky.

Easy traced Deena's gaze – Fez, a muscular boy with the beginnings of a moustache. Fez's father had just joined the board of Gunman Reds as a director, making him one of Dad's bosses. His family had moved into one of the grand old houses that perched on the edge of Highbury Fields. Fez was a little older than Easy. He was already signed up with the Reds, and in a couple of weeks he'd be away to Nuvillage, their countryside training centre. Fez thought he was good, but actually the only thing that raised him above average was a strong kick, a big mouth and an even bigger ego to go with it.

With a couple of his teammates, Fez blocked Easy's path. He nodded towards Gunman's cannon in the sky. Every five minutes, all but two of the spokes on the cannon wheel blinked off. These were the hands of a clock – the clock they always played to. People said it was visible on the very fringes of London. For those closer by, a digital readout on the cannon's barrel gave the time every sixty seconds. As Easy stared, it flashed. *16:43*. Just 17 minutes to go.

'Forget it!' Fez chuckled. 'You ain't catching us now.'

'Oh … right!' Easy's tone oozed with sarcasm. 'You're *so* confident. That must be why you're trying to stall us.' He pushed his way through the gathering players. 'I *don't* think so.' Around him, teammates hooted, laughed and scattered to their positions.

Fez sneered. 'Yeah, like we really need to stall … *ball in play!*' His kick soared out to the wing. He set off running. 'Four goals in fifteen minutes, genius – let's see you do it!'

Boys from both teams took off across the grass, but Easy jogged into open space, scanning the field, taking stock. With everyone chasing the ball there was little room for skill or technique, only the biggest or maybe the fastest prevailed. Doubling their score in so little time demanded *tactics*. Scant hope of that. Where was their captain?

Easy stopped in his tracks and stared. A familiar figure was making its way along the path towards the onlookers – Dad. It wasn't unusual for him to come by after work, but recently he'd been working late. Easy watched: Trix and Deena turned to greet him under the big old tree. Dad spoke quickly in return, his expression was stern. He pointed towards home.

'*Easy!*'

Easy twisted. Out of the chaos of stumbling, struggling players, the ball came curling through the air. He trapped it, turned towards the goal and began to run.

'Go, Easy, go!' Teammates' voices urged him on. 'Run with it, Easy!' But though he was heading, full pelt, towards the goal, his eyes kept darting to the sidelines. Trix and Deena had set off towards the house. Something was *wrong*.

Dad beckoned. *'Leave it!'* There was urgency – a shakiness in his voice.

'What ...' Still dribbling, Easy swerved towards him.

'Just leave it. Leave the ball.' Dad gesticulated. 'Come *on!*'

'What's wrong?'

Dad's face was stony. His eyes flickered nervously towards the spectators. 'We have to go home – now.'

'Man on!'

Easy turned too late. The impact sent him sprawling to the ground.

'Cheers!' Hooking the ball away, Fez took off down the field.

Easy scrambled to his feet.

'Easy ...' Dad's voice snapped. *'Leave it!'*

On either side of Mum, Deena and Trix fidgeted restlessly on the sofa. Easy half-sat, half-leant against the arm, fiddling with a loose thread.

A walk home from the Fields with Dad was usually something he relished – the two of them alone together. If Dad dropped by on his way from work, he never came without a ball. Kicking it back and forth,

16

the pair of them would chat and exchange stories about their day. But with Dad working so late recently, these walks home together had become something of a rare pleasure.

Today had been different. The path under the trees had seemed way too long and, in the dying light, too dark, too damp, too chilly. Today there had been no ball, and an awkward silence had stretched between them.

Easy shuddered, glanced across at his father.

Stony-faced, as he had been all the way home, Dad made a nervous coughing sound. 'What I have to say is going to be a shock.' He shook his head wearily. 'But there isn't an easy way to do this ...'

Trix and Deena shuffled on the sofa.

'I've ... resigned.'

The room froze.

Dad nodded slowly. 'Gunman Reds have been my team since I was a boy. *Years* as a supporter, two years as a player, five as assistant coach, eight as chief scout ...' His voice wavered. 'Not any more.' A heavy sigh. 'There, I've said it.'

The girls exchanged glances.

'Unfortunately, no job means no salary.' Dad's arms fell limply against his sides. 'From today we're a family without income.'

Mum's lips pressed tight together; she clasped and unclasped her hands, then, becoming self-conscious, buried them in the folds of her skirt.

'Our lifestyle has never been extravagant,' said Dad, 'but we don't have a lot of savings. I'm sorry ...'

He shook his head. '… it's all a bit abrupt, but … some changes we're going to have to make straight away.' His apologetic eyes flitted from face to face. 'Starting, I'm afraid, with where we live.'

'What!?' Easy practically fell from his perch.

'We have to *move*?' Deena was on her feet. 'To a smaller house, you mean?'

Dad frowned. 'More likely an apartment.'

'An *apartment*!' Deena's face was a picture of horror. 'Sharing rooms?'

'Oh God, *no* …' Trix looked mortified. 'Please – no!'

Dad shrugged. 'We'll have to see.' His voice betrayed anxiety. 'I need to sit down with our accountant and go through everything.'

Easy watched a vein throbbing on Dad's forehead. Dad usually made light of even the grimmest situations. Things had to be bad – he'd never looked like this.

The shocks weren't over. As Easy lay in his bed, staring up at the faces of the Gunman Reds 1st XI plastered across his bedroom ceiling, the door opened. Dad nodded and seated himself at the end of the bed. Easy pushed himself up against the pillows and waited for his father to speak.

'As soon as we've moved,' Dad lifted his head, 'I'll be going away.'

'Away?'

'Just short visits, but I … there are some old contacts, people I need to visit.'

'To try and find work?'

Dad half-shrugged, half-nodded.

'You shouldn't have to go far, with your experience and reputation.'

'I'm afraid it's not that simple.' Dad shook his head. 'Not any more. Things have changed. There are going to be some difficult times ahead.' He sighed. 'You, me ... Mum ... the girls – as a family we have to make a special effort not to let stuff come between us.'

Easy nodded, uncertain what he was agreeing to. The silence returned.

Dad frowned, picked up a cushion and fiddled with it. 'Easy ...'

'Yes, Dad?'

'You have to do something for me.'

'Uh-huh.'

'I want you to ...' Dad coughed to clear his throat. '... I need you to give up playing football.'

'What!' Easy laughed uneasily. 'Give up? How d'you mean?'

'No more football.'

'You're kidding – right?'

Dad's face remained grave. Slowly, he shook his head.

Easy clutched the duvet. He was trembling. He felt like he was sinking. 'Seriously – you're really asking me to *quit*?'

Dad's nod was solemn. 'No playing for a team at your new school, no joining local clubs, no kickabouts, not even kicking a ball against a wall.' The eyes were hard steel. 'Not litter, not leaves, not sticks nor stones – *nothing*. No kicking, full stop.'

3

SUNDAY

Tomorrow would make it three weeks – the most miserable three weeks of his life.

At the end of the cul-de-sac a group of boys played makeshift five-a-side between two garage doors. The space was tiny and potholed, but in his wanderings about the area it wasn't the craziest place he'd spotted a football being kicked. No pitches, no parks; tiny yards, rough-surfaced playgrounds, and only the skinniest patches of grass. This new world was not football-friendly, but there was no shortage of games. Easy paused, glanced around, then propped himself against a wall. He'd watch the game … just for a few minutes.

A few days throwing stuff away, packing and saying goodbyes to friends. Then off. It had been as quick as that – Dad had managed to find them somewhere straight away. It wasn't a house, it wasn't Highbury, it was rented and only short-term, but at least it was still north of the river and still up on the Heights, not Downtown, not in the crowded, polluted City or Southside. There was no view – just another apartment block opposite and the narrowest strip of grass. But he was lucky – he still had a room to himself; Trix and Deena were now forced to share.

'*Goal!*'

'Was never.'

'Was!'

'Don't be stupid – it was *way* out.'

With a sigh, Easy turned away from the boys and their game. He knew where he was heading …

Dad had told them they'd soon settle in, but nothing would ever be the same. How could it be? They'd all grown up living in one place. Now, suddenly, they found themselves somewhere shabbier. They'd had to leave behind their friends and had to start being 'careful' with money. Highbury was out of bounds to them all, as were their old friends.

Mum looked worn. The girls were irritable over sharing a room and Deena bore him the biggest grudge ever because he had a room of his own. Since the move, Dad had been away more than he'd been home. When he returned, he too looked tired and drawn. He seemed distracted. He locked himself away in his study with his console.

But topping everything else: *no more football*. If a ball came his way on the street or in the playground, he was not allowed even to return it. Just walk on by. If he spotted a game underway, he was supposed to move on. He wasn't just forbidden to kick, he wasn't to head, chest or exhibit any other kind of football skill. He wasn't even to wear his Gunman Reds gear. The ban was total.

All his life he had lived and breathed football. Before the recent upheaval, he had believed himself to be one of the best. Dad had never expressed anything but confidence in his ability; he had always reassured him he'd have a place at Gunman Reds' training camp when he came of age. Becoming a pro, playing for the lst XI and fulfilling his father's ambitions – that had been his only dream. Now the rug had been snatched from under his feet. What was he supposed to think?

What could be Dad's reasons? Mum may have had an inkling, but she wasn't letting on. Trix's theory was that Dad was keeping Easy's talent under wraps because he wanted to get some other club to sign him up. Deena however was much more cynical.

'There can only be one explanation,' she'd informed him, 'Dad, or Gunman Reds, possibly both, have discovered there's something wrong with you, some incurable condition which means you're not up to being a pro. It happens all the time – a young player looks promising, he goes for his regular medical, something shows up and presto – his career's over.' Deena had smiled. 'It's probably something terminal. But rather than give you the shock news straight out, Dad's decided to create some elaborate mystery about why you aren't allowed to play. He's saving your feelings.'

Not for one moment had he believed her, of course, but he couldn't push the doubts from his mind. What was going on? Why had Dad banned him from playing football and then left him in the dark? On more than one occasion it'd occurred to him that he might sneak into his parents' room, hack into Dad's personal console and find out *the truth*.

Last week, he had actually gone as far as slipping into their room while Dad was taking a shower. The slim black bag Dad always carried had been sitting on his desk, still unopened from the latest trip. A guilty rummage among the papers had revealed just some handwritten notes and letters to do with the Category P list and performance-enhancers. Nothing he could make any sense of.

Dad's personal console and discs might have revealed more, had they not been tightly protected by passwords, encryptions and codes. Hacking was fantasy, no point even trying. Anyway, by then he was feeling guilty about the snooping he'd already done.

As familiar streets opened out into Highbury Fields, and the red neon cannon came into view, Easy felt his heart gallop. How lucky they had been – living here, with this wide open space so close at hand. Reaching for his hood, he pulled it up over his head and down low, shading his eyes.

A kickabout game was under way – the usual suspects running ragtag across the grass. Keeping close to the trees, he made his way nearer. Could he risk one last game? What could be the harm? Anyway, how was Dad ever going to find out? He was probably on the other side of the country.

Still some distance from the spot where most of the spectators were gathered, Easy froze. Directly in front of him, a lone figure stood beneath a tree. The person's hair was concealed beneath a cap, but their jacket, a quilted silver effort, was exactly like one Deena had received for her birthday. She hadn't stopped bragging about how exclusive it was. He moved closer, till he could read the lettering on the back. *Sylvia Andersen, 21st Century Fashions.*

'Go on, Fez, *whack* it! Show them what you're made of.'

Deena's voice! It really was her. Turning on his heel, Easy hurried away towards the cover of trees.

He'd not hung about long. There hadn't been much point. He'd recognized his sister, why let her recognize him? But what a turn up for the books! Deena, of all people, sneaking back home to watch the football. And shouting for Fez! He should have guessed.

As he made his way back home towards the new apartment block, the streets grew steadily busier, noisier, smellier – clogged with vehicles, nose to tail, crawling at a snail's pace. The spaces between buildings grew smaller till they disappeared altogether. The pavements were becoming more and more crowded.

Suddenly, there was shouting and commotion up ahead.

'Hey!'

'Sorry, mate.'

'Ow!'

'Sorry, missus.'

'Look where you're going!'

'Mind out!'

Before he could step out of the way, Easy was barged sideways by a tornado. Dribbling a football through the legs of pedestrians, a boy with a cap pulled down over his eyes charged, helter-skelter, weaving and bobbing along the crowded sidewalk. Behind him others shoved and barged, shouting and laughing, as they gave chase.

In their wake they left a trail of outraged pedestrians, shaking their fists, cursing the young, bemoaning inadequate modern parenting.

Recovering his balance, Easy spun on his heel and set off in pursuit of the pursuers. In his path, disgruntled shoppers shook fists as they stooped to pick up scattered groceries and dropped shopping trolleys, a large policeman struggled to get up off his behind, businessmen muttered angrily and straightened their suits, mothers fussed over traumatized babies. Apologizing as he skipped and dodged, Easy pushed his legs faster and faster.

Somewhere behind, the policeman's whistle began to blow. The running boys spilled out into the traffic. As the boy with the cap dodged between the slow-moving vehicles, he turned to mock his pursuers, goading them on. Cars honked their horns, drivers leant out of windows and added their voices to the racket.

Suddenly, he had doubled back. Jumping tackles, the boy with the cap chipped the ball on to a van roof, scrambled up behind it and down the other side. Straight into Easy who had seen the boy coming and, at the last minute, side-stepped, snaring the ball.

'Oi!' Twisting his cap back from his eyes, the boy turned and lunged.

'You!' Easy stared at the freckled face.

'I'd close my mouth if I were you.' The boy grinned, the ball safely back between his feet. 'Sorry, mate ...' He turned. 'Too slow!' Sprinting away, he dodged between the cars.

'*Hey!*' Easy took off after him. 'I *know* you ... I saw you at the Inter-Schools ...'

Freckle-face turned down a side street. Now Easy was at the front of the chasing pack. 'I can take the ball off you,' he panted, 'every time!' He pushed his legs to go faster. 'Come on ...' he yelled, 'you can't run for ever. Turn and face me!'

But the boy kept going, ball at his feet, weaving in and out between cars and pedestrians. At the end of the street, he cut left. Easy and the pack followed. On either side, high brick buildings backed on to the road. Suddenly, the boy had the ball in his hands and was legging it, two and three steps at a time, up a black iron fire-escape.

Easy followed. Behind him, the chasing boys grunted. Seconds later, their grunts were echoed by cheers from the roof of the building. Faces appeared.

'Jordan! Jordan! Jordan!'

Easy gasped for air. He was gaining on the boy, tier by tier. Ten steps to a tier ... two tiers to a floor ... Footsteps rang on the tiers below as the other boys fell behind. Fourteen tiers: the seventh floor. Fifteen. Sixteen. Easy was nearly close enough to reach out and grab the boy ...

'Jordan!'

Suddenly, the fire-escape opened out on to a big flat roof.

'Jordan!' Boys in an assortment of football strips cheered and punched the air.

Flinging the ball over their heads, the boy in the cap turned to Easy. He leant against the rail, clutching his chest. 'You're *fast* …' he panted. 'I'd remember you, if we'd ever played.' He held out his hand. 'I'm Jordan. Where've you been hiding?'

'Easy …' Easy fought to slow his breathing. 'I remember you … Inter-Schools Championship … two years ago.'

Jordan stared blankly. 'Before we got knocked out.'

Easy nodded. 'I played for Highbury then. But now I live round here.'

'Highbury to here?' Jordan pulled a face and gave him a consoling pat on the back. 'Bummer. That's a sad story. What happened – bad luck?'

Easy shrugged. 'Something like that.' Behind him, the fire-escape clanged as the first of the chasing boys staggered, breathless, on to the roof. Groans of exhaustion followed.

Jordan nodded towards the rooftop. 'Space is one of the many things this neighbourhood doesn't have a lot of. To get a game round here – you've got to be enterprising.' He stamped hard on the asphalt and smiled mischievously. 'This building's a college; it's empty weekends. And when the caretaker and his missus do their weekly shop …' He chuckled. '… we get our kickabout. Come on!'

4

FETCHER

The players formed themselves into two teams. A couple of them, Easy realized, were girls.

'Give or take the odd change here and there, we always play with the same sides,' said Jordan. He and the taller boy everyone referred to as 'Afro' were the captains. 'Afro's team has more good players,' explained Jordan, 'to compensate for my all-round footballing genius.' Smiling impishly, he turned to Afro. 'I've lost track – how many games since you guys beat us?'

Sour-faced, Afro muttered incomprehensibly.

'Sorry?' Jordan persisted. 'Didn't quite catch that.'

'Nine,' grunted Afro.

Jordan turned to his teammates. 'Let's see if we can make it an even ten.'

His team cheered and punched the air.

Jordan glanced over at Easy, eyes narrowed. 'Could be a tough one today. This new boy Easy looks like he plans to make things difficult for us.'

With a sudden horrible stomach-lurching feeling, Easy realized what a trap he'd set for himself. He wasn't supposed to be playing football – he'd made Dad a promise. But like a fool, when he'd seen the boys chasing Jordan he'd let his excitement run away with him. If he walked away now, he'd be laughed at and ridiculed.

Afro tossed a coin.

'Heads!' yelled Jordan.

The coin bounced to a stop on the asphalt. Afro crouched to examine it. 'Tails.'

Jordan shrugged. 'You need all the luck you can get.' He pointed to the far end. 'We'll take that side. May the best team win!'

Afro beckoned his team.

Joining the others in an excited huddle around their captain, Easy felt their glances – sizing him up.

Afro nodded. 'Where d'you like to play? Up front?'

'Er ...' Easy stuttered. He sensed the hope and anticipation of his teammates waver and evaporate. 'I ... er, I like the midfield,' he mumbled. 'Central.'

Afro glared. 'You don't sound too certain. We could do without a liability.'

Easy felt the accusation in his captain's eyes. 'I'll do my best.' It wasn't quite the truth. But no one would guess. He stared back.

'Let's hope that's enough.' Afro pushed out his chest. 'Right. Easy goes in central midfield. Baz, you move up front with me.' Making a fist, he smacked it into his palm. 'Let's do it!'

Players dispersed to their positions.

Afro took the kick, passing back to Baz. Baz flicked it on to Easy.

Easy paused on the ball, scanning the pitch; his teammates moved forward, zigzagging in an attempt to throw off their markers. Surely there'd be no harm in a couple of decent passes just to start off with? No one was going to draw conclusions from that.

Jordan had disposed of his cap: his short rust-coloured dreadlocks, freed of their restraint, rose up in a wild spiky crown. The grin had vanished. 'Yaaaaagh!' He charged forward, a battle-hungry warrior.

Easy danced the ball between his feet as Jordan hurtled in for the tackle. Jordan snarled. At the last moment Easy sidestepped, glanced up the field and lofted the ball.

Jordan swivelled in time to see the high arc of Easy's pass. Floating over half the length of the pitch, it dropped steeply. Easy was already running, his feet pounding on the rough dark asphalt. Honed instinct. *Follow up the pass. Support the attack.*

Afro, perfectly positioned to receive, headed the ball across the width of the pitch. Two boys jumped, Easy recognized one as a teammate. Now a gaggle of players fought to take possession of the ball.

Yelling, Jordan rushed to join the action. As the ball was hoofed clear, he was there to take advantage. But before he could gather speed or make a pass, Easy was on his case, harassing with his feet.

'Get out of here!' Jordan kept possession of the ball with deft footwork. He grinned, amused at Easy's doggedness and the little rivalry developing between them. 'You got lucky before,' chuckled Jordan.

Easy caught the ball a heavy sideswipe. Cannoning

off both players, it ricocheted up, soaring, then fell from sight. Groans and cries of *'First Drop!'* echoed from the players as they rushed to the edge of the roof and crowded against the mesh fence.

Jordan pointed down at the tiny ball, rolling to a stop in the yard, eight floors below. 'You had last touch.'

'I never!' Easy glared. 'That went out off your shins.'

'Did not!'

'Did!'

'Whatever ...' Jordan dismissed the argument with a wave of his hand. 'I'll concede the throw-in. But there's no escaping the fact that it was your clumsy punt that sent the ball into the yard. That, I'm afraid, was your *first drop.'*

'First drop?' Easy scowled. 'What's that? What's all this *first drop* business?'

'I should have explained.' Afro appeared, clutching a ball. 'Because it's such a pain when the ball goes over the edge, we have a rule: whoever kicks the ball over the most times in one game has to do the fetching for the following game.' He flipped the ball to Easy. 'We have four balls. When the third one goes down, the fetcher has to go and collect all the balls from the yard.'

'So while the fetcher is off gathering balls,' said Easy, 'the game continues with one side a player short?'

Afro nodded. 'Today it's Marky.' He pointed to a pale skinny lad, playing in defence for Jordan's team.

'So balls over the edge could be to our advantage?' said Easy.

Afro shrugged. 'Teams often play better when they're one player down.'

31

'There's one other thing,' said Jordan. 'If anyone gets three drops in a game, they become the fetcher, taking over from whoever's current. On their third drop they have to go down to the yard even if it's just for the one ball.' He patted the ball Easy was holding. 'Watch how you kick that thing.' He grinned. 'Only two drops to go!'

Easy returned the grin. Jordan had given him an idea.

Following the throw-in, the pace and ferocity of the game quickened. Easy's mind was made up: he was already breaking his promise, he owed it to Dad to at least get out of the game as quickly as possible. Each time the ball came his way he did his best to help his team on their way, but whenever the opportunity arose he took the ball towards the edge or made a pass to the wing that was harder and higher than required. Before too long he had notched his second drop with a wild *blaster*.

Jordan's team had gone 1–0 up. Afro was growing irritable. 'Come on!' he barked.' We've got one more man than them.'

'For what it's worth,' muttered Baz.

'Yeah.' Afro scowled at Easy. 'Sharpen up, or at least do us all a favour and stay away from the edge!'

Baz placed the ball on the centre spot. 'Come on!' he yelled, taking the kick. 'We ought to be thrashing them!'

The ball flew out to the wing, low and controlled, not like the passes Easy had been making. The winger took the ball on the run, dribbling round one … two … *three* of Jordan's players. He passed inside. Afro was there waiting. He chipped to Baz. With a quick change of step, Baz volleyed. Like a rocket, the ball smashed into the fencing and bounced back. Easy charged and, flinging himself, booted the ball with every ounce of his strength.

As the ball soared high over the fencing, Easy hit the asphalt hard. Palms, elbows and knees stung with a pain he knew he'd regret later. Looking up, he was just in time to glimpse the ball dropping from sight. He struggled to his feet.

Afro swore loudly. The other players fell about laughing. 'What the heck's wrong with you?' Afro towered over Easy, fists clenched. 'Are you some kind of *retard*?'

Easy winced and straightened up. 'Everyone makes mistakes.'

'Yeah, some more than most.' Afro moved in close, bringing his face right up against Easy's. He sneered. 'Well, now you pay for yours.'

Easy winced again. Afro's breath was rotten.

Players gathered. Pushing Afro gently, Jordan stepped between the two boys. He grinned at Easy. 'Not a bad start.'

Afro snorted. 'You kidding?' He jabbed a finger in Easy's chest. 'Take my advice – forget about football altogether.'

'That's a bit harsh!' Jordan laughed and shook his head. 'Afro's just sore because his team are behind yet again.' He patted Easy on the shoulder. 'You want to watch that right foot of yours, though. Maybe you should try wearing a lead-lined boot or something.' He winked. 'A bit of weight might take the edge off it.'

'I'm just excited.' Easy lowered his eyes, embarrassed by the lie. 'I haven't played for a while. I always tend to kick the ball too hard at first.'

Jamming two fingers between his teeth, Jordan let out a piercing whistle. A ball came flying. He caught it and held it out in front of Easy. 'This is ball number four.' Jordan nodded towards the yard below. 'The other three are down there. All kicked by you. I'm afraid that makes you the *fetcher*.'

Easy shrugged. 'A rule's a rule.' He glanced at Afro. 'Perhaps you'll do better without me.'

'Perhaps?' Afro grunted. 'Don't hurry back.' He turned and walked away, barking orders to his players.

Jordan chuckled. 'He's moody at the best of times. Such fun when he's losing.'

Easy smiled. 'You haven't seen me play my best.'

'There's plenty of time,' said Jordan. 'I'm sure I will.' He tossed the ball between his palms. 'The game's waiting. I'd better take this throw.'

Easy jogged his way towards the fire-escape, the sounds of the game ringing in his ears. As he reached the top step, he turned for one last glance. All the players except one were facing the action at the far end. Giving a discreet wave, Jordan turned and ran to join the fray.

5

SET UP

'Hiya, little brother.'

Ignoring the provocation, Easy dropped his school bag on the floor and headed for the fridge.

'Mum's left a note.' Deena slid a writing pad across the kitchen table. 'Something about doing part-time cleaning – she's taken Trix with her. There's chicken in the micro. Dad's train's supposed to get in around ten.' Deena fiddled with the end of a braid. 'So – what did you get up to yesterday?'

'Went for a wander.' Easy filled a glass with orange. 'Still finding my way around.' He drank.

'Discover anything interesting?'

Easy shrugged. 'The area's pretty much all the same. A bit more lively round the shopping centre. But, apart from that – just apartment blocks.'

'Yeah.' Deena's top lip lifted in a sneer. 'It's not the most exciting place to live, is it? Meet anyone, did you? Make any new friends?'

'Nah.' Easy sat down opposite her. Deena was probing – what was she after? He shrugged again. 'Not really.'

'What d'you mean?' Deena studied her brother. 'Why d'you keep shrugging? Either you did or you didn't.'

'I spotted a couple of boys I recognized from my school.' Easy glanced away. 'That's all.'

'You're such a liar, Easy Linker.'

'*What?*'

'You heard me.' Rubber squealed against linoleum as Deena shoved back her chair. She stood. 'You're a fraud – you make out you're such an innocent, such a goody-two-shoes.' She did a balletic skip. 'Mum and Dad think the sun shines out of your ... *hmm*, but I know the truth. I know what you're really like.'

'What are you blathering on about?' Easy followed his sister through to the open-plan living area – lounge, hallway, dining room.

'Oh, yes ...' Deena flopped on an enormous cushion. 'Quite an accomplished deceiver.'

'What?'

'But you've never fooled me.'

Easy frowned.

Deena picked up the remote. The screen flashed into life. 'What have you got to hide, bro?'

On the screen the family homepage appeared. The cursor glided to Deena's icon; the screen filled with a picture of her face. 'Keep out!' snarled the image. 'This zone is *private*. Password entry only.'

Deena tapped buttons on the remote. The screen flashed to her homepage – a battalion of files. 'If you don't want people knowing what you're up to,' she smiled, 'you need to be a little more discreet.' On screen, she moved the cursor to an icon of a magnifying glass. It was labelled *Investigations*. The screen refilled: more files; the cursor lit on one labelled *Easy*.

Easy felt himself tensing. He rubbed the back of his neck.

'Rule number one,' said Deena. 'If you don't want somebody finding out what you've been up to on the net, don't use a shared access point.' The cursor moved to the top right-hand corner of the screen – the *Commands* pull-down menu. Pointing the remote, Deena dragged the cursor down the list of commands till it got to *Recall Previous*.

Easy chewed at his bottom lip. *Where was this leading to?*

'I always do this when I log on,' said Deena. 'It gives the last five commands – saves time, if you always use the same ones.' She smiled again – pure, unashamed smugness. 'Of course, if someone else has been on before you, you get to discover what they've been up to …'

Easy held her gaze.

'So when I saw you'd been doing a spot of net-shopping …' Deena pointed the remote. '… I was curious.'

Easy shrugged. 'So …?'

'So …' Deena turned to the screen. '… what's my brother buying from World-Mart?'

Easy glanced at the screen. Froze.

'Why would he be making payment directly from his own account? Unless he didn't want Mum and

Dad to know? Why would he do that?' Deena's eyebrows arched expectantly. She pointed to the screen. 'Thirty millilitres of Drug Inc.'s product No. 1074. Look that up, and what do we find ... Quick-Heal.'

Easy squirmed. 'What's wrong with Quick-Heal? I got a graze.'

'You get a graze – you let it heal, *naturally*. That stuff's meant for people who need to *disguise* their wounds, because of their job or whatever.' With surprising speed, Deena jumped up from the cushion. 'Let's take a look.'

Easy drew back.

'It's obvious you're hiding something.' Lunging suddenly, Deena grabbed his arm. 'You never usually wear long sleeves.' She gripped him tight, tugging his sleeve up to the elbow. 'Aha ... no graze, no scabbing, *hmmm* ...' She prodded. 'But I bet there's still bruis–'

Easy flinched. '*Ow!*' His free hand clamped on his sister's wrist and squeezed *hard*.

'*Ow!*' Deena winced. 'You're hurting me!' Her arm went limp. 'Easy – you're *hurting* me!

He eased his grip.

She jerked away. 'Why do you need to hide a graze?'

'What business is it of yours?'

Deena shrugged, massaging her wrist. 'You're my brother ... I *care*.' She glanced at his legs. 'That elbow isn't your only injury.' Her voice softened. 'You think no one notices? I've seen you limping.'

'How sweet ...' Easy gave a sarcastic smile. '... so

worried about me.' She didn't fool him. 'Come off it, Deena! You go to all that trouble delving into my private business. And now you're asking me to believe you're *concerned*! You?' He snorted. 'You *know* why I had to hide my grazes.'

Deena shook her head. 'Could be all sorts of reasons. Tell me why, and I promise not to say a word.'

'Yeah, right. My caring sister.'

'Don't believe me, then.' Deena shrugged. 'It's no skin off my nose.' She folded her arms. 'But you'd better tell, or I'll grass you up about the Quick-Heal.'

'The Deena we all know and love.' Easy scowled. 'You would too.'

Deena nodded and held out her hand. 'I give you my word: I won't if you tell me why you covered up the grazes.'

'She gives me her word!' Easy sighed. 'That makes me feel a *whole* lot better.' He considered the outstretched hand. 'Don't exactly have much choice, do I?'

Deena smiled – pleased with herself. 'No.'

Easy pushed away the proffered palm. 'I got them playing football.'

Deena's jaw dropped. '*Football?*' It was practically a shriek. 'After Dad made such a big thing about how you *mustn't*?'

Easy shrugged. 'There was this boy, Jordan.'

Deena's eyebrows lifted, expectantly. 'And …?'

'Forget it.' Easy slumped. 'You wouldn't understand.'

'You're probably right,' said Deena. '*Try* me.'

'He's the best player I've ever seen.' Easy glanced at his sister. Her face showed no emotion. 'I know I told Dad I wouldn't play, but … I had to. Just this once.'

'I can't believe it …' The shocked face again. 'You played a whole game?'

'No way!' said Easy. 'I kept thinking about Dad. I only played for a short time. I had to play badly to get out of the game.' He shook his head, forlornly. 'It wasn't fun. They ended up mocking me. But Jordan sensed I had more than I was showing – he never said a word.'

'But with all the pressure Dad's been under!' Deena was practically shouting, arms akimbo. 'And he specifically asked you not to play!'

'Out of my face!' Easy pushed his sister away. 'You can get down off your high horse!'

'What?'

'You've disobeyed him too.'

'What!' Real shock. 'I have *not*!'

'Liar!' Easy jabbed Deena with his index finger. 'You've been going back to Highbury – after Dad asked us to stay away.'

'Don't be ridiculous!' Deena shook her head furiously. Her eyes flashed. 'That's a lie … that's a *lie*!'

Easy spoke softly. 'You know it isn't.'

'Why would *I* go to Highbury?'

'Come off it, Deena! You and – ' Some small sound caught Easy's ear. He spun round. 'Dad!'

The bedroom door was open, the room in darkness.

From the shadows, Todd Linker's pale grey eyes flitted from daughter to son and back again. He shuffled, blinking, out into the light. 'So much for keeping the noise down, Deena. Little chance of sleep with you two around.'

Easy glared at his sister. She had *known*! She had known Dad was home all along! She had known Dad was in the bedroom trying to sleep. She had set the whole thing up. Dad had heard everything.

'So ...' Todd Linker folded his arms and sighed. 'This is what goes on behind my back.'

Easy watched his sister bite her lip. She hadn't been expecting his revelation about her visit to Highbury.

Dad moved closer. He stood between them. 'Deena, is it true? Have you been back?'

'*No*, Dad!' Deeply offended. 'He's just saying that to make himself look better.' She turned. 'You should be ashamed of yourself, you little liar. '

'Liar yourself!'

'Am not!'

'I *saw* you!' Easy lunged. Dad's solid forearm barred his path and held him back. Easy scowled, turned away.

'You must've been mistaken.' Deena's voice was calm and confident 'I haven't been back.'

Suddenly, Easy was filled with doubt. *Had it been Deena?* He'd never actually seen her, it had just been the jacket. He tried to remember some other tell-tale detail, but none came to mind. Perhaps he was wrong.

With his finger Dad raised Deena's chin. His eyes scanned hers for truth. 'People make mistakes.' He rested his hand on her shoulder. 'If you say you didn't go back, I believe you.' He turned. 'Easy and I need to have a little talk …' The look was stern. 'Could you pop out for a while?' He held out his card. 'Get me a paper?'

'I suppose.' Deena made no attempt to hide her misgivings but, as she passed Easy, there was a twinkle in her eye. Her plan had worked. He was about to be crucified.

6

CATEGORY P

The front door slammed.

Dad turned. 'So – what have you got to say for yourself?'

'Sorry …' Easy stared at his trainers. 'I tried really hard … but football's the one thing in my life.' He glanced up. 'I couldn't do it. Staying away was too difficult.'

Dad's face was expressionless. 'How many times have you played since you promised not to?'

'Just the once.'

'And this boy who was so good you just had to play against him – what was his name?'

'Jordan.'

'Jordan Snapes?'

Easy nodded. 'You know him?'

'Gunman Reds have had their eye on him for a while.' Dad frowned. 'Did he mention anything?'

'Yeah – he told me he's had interest from both Gunman and New Spurs. His family are solid New Spurs though.'

Dad shook his head. 'Team loyalty's a luxury

43

people in this neighbourhood can't afford. He'll go to the money. Any scouts watching the game?'

'Unlikely,' said Easy, 'unless they had lenses. We were up on a rooftop.'

'Resourceful.' Dad sighed, pulled up a chair and sat down, thumb and forefinger massaging his brow.

Easy waited. Something important was coming.

'Sit down.' Dad gestured towards the cushion in front of him. He waited for Easy to settle. 'My decision not to explain stuff – resigning from Gunman Reds, the ban on you playing football and all that – perhaps it wasn't the right one.' He clasped his hands, resting his elbows on his knees. 'I can see now: without any explanation, the ban must have seemed, well – very unfair.'

'Very,' echoed Easy.

'The temptation to play must have been overwhelming,' said Dad. He shifted his weight, leant forward. 'What I'm going to tell you must be kept totally secret.' The voice dropped. 'You must repeat this to no one, *no one* – not even your mother. Do you understand?'

Easy nodded.

Dad's expression was grave. 'The secrecy is vital, Easy. Lives are in danger.' He brought his face down close. 'I'm telling you this because *yours* is one of them.'

'*My* life?' Easy felt his skin prickle. 'In danger from who?'

'Football.' Dad's eyes measured his reaction. 'Football is killing its young stars.'

Easy's throat dried. *'Killing* them?'

Dad nodded. 'Poisoning them with so-called performance-enhancers and all the other chemical rubbish clubs are pumping into their players. Trying to squeeze out extra effort.' His voice was pure disdain. '"For that winning edge."'

'But enhancers are regulated now,' said Easy. 'Aren't the ones on the P list meant to be safe, just like the vitamins, minerals and all the other supplements that have been okayed by IFFA's laboratories?'

'Safe?' Dad gave a derisory snort. 'How would anyone know? Some of the drugs on that list have only recently been developed. We don't even know what the short-term effects are, let alone the long-term consequences.' His face darkened. 'Oh, but I've got to hand it to IFFA, they've done a good job of convincing people.'

'You don't believe them?'

Dad shook his head. 'IFFA are in cahoots with the clubs. They've been suppressing the evidence of side-effects for so long they've almost forgotten they're doing it. I've heard of secret reports of problems with several of the enhancers on the Category P list. I've seen the evidence myself.'

Easy felt the skin of his scalp tighten. These were the enhancers he would be taking if he were a pro. 'Why would IFFA do that?'

'Because they are the governing authority; they need to be seen to be in control. There's no problem if clubs are all conforming to the rules and players only take enhancers from the list.' Dad's eyes narrowed.

'Why did IFFA come up with Category P?'

Easy considered the question. The issue had been covered daily on the sports channels. 'Because clubs have been developing so many new enhancers, IFFA's laboratory tests couldn't keep up. They had no way of knowing whether players were enhanced or not.'

'Right.' Dad nodded. 'And if new, undetectable enhancers gave them the edge before, why not now?'

Easy shifted uncomfortably on the cushion. 'Are you going to take your evidence to the authorities?'

'It's not that simple. IFFA *is* the authority – the *world* authority. It has enormous influence. So far, they, the clubs and their corporation backers have been very thorough in making sure no one inside the game speaks out. They couldn't carry that off without serious support and co-operation elsewhere.'

'Outside the game?' said Easy. 'You mean police, politicians and those sort of people?'

Dad nodded. 'Along with journalists, broadcasters, judges, magistrates and lawyers.'

'But surely, if enhancers are making players ill …'

'They don't get ill straight away. These days players are given a whole cocktail of substances – some of them enhancers, some of them pacifiers – mind-control drugs, some of them narcotics to keep the side-effects at bay.'

'This is going on in *all* the clubs?'

Dad nodded solemnly. 'Looks that way.'

'And no player has been prepared to speak out?'

'While they're under contract, the clubs have too

much control.' Dad frowned. 'And these days, players are signing up for *life*. Playing spans get shorter and shorter, but you're still on their payroll long after your playing days are over. A couple of the older, retired players: Damon Huckerby, Brad Kowalski, I reckon they might have had something to say.'

'But they're both ... '

Dad nodded.

Easy felt suddenly cold. They were *dead*. 'Brad crashed his car and Damon died in hospital – wasn't there some story about a technical fault in the life-support equipment?' Easy shivered. 'You're not saying they were ...'

'Helped to die?' Dad shrugged. 'I can't speak for Brad. But I knew Damon, of course, and *he* was definitely unhappy about the system. He'd been sounding off about how the club's enhancer programme had been responsible for his tumours and various ailments. For a long time Gunman Reds had been trying to placate him, trying to get him to keep quiet, but he wouldn't give it up.'

'I can't believe it!' Easy slumped. 'You're suggesting ... that's ... '

'Too terrible to contemplate?' Dad sighed. 'Well, now you're getting the picture.' His face looked tired. 'There's something else you should know, something that puts it in context.' He massaged his brow. 'The year you were born, I was still a player. I wanted to guarantee a deal for you, should you ever want to play.' He bowed his head. 'I signed a contract giving Gunman Reds first refusal on you.'

Easy felt his heart flutter – it always did at the thought of playing for Gunman Reds. But he knew by his father's tone, a 'first refusal' wasn't something that should fill him with joy.

'In theory, they could make you play for them, even if you don't want to.'

'What! That's ridiculous! No one can *make* you play.'

'Uh-huh – you'd think so, wouldn't you. But I've heard stories of clubs doing exactly that.' Dad paused. 'Perhaps now you can understand why it's been so important for us to move away.'

'That's why you didn't want me having anything to do with football. You thought Gunman Reds might get word of where we were living?'

Dad nodded. 'I know every boy dreams of being signed up on his birthday. You're just going to have to wait a little longer. If we stay in this sort of neighbourhood, moving flats from time to time, it should make it pretty tricky for the club's agents to track us down. Hopefully, enough evidence will have been gathered by then to expose this whole corrupt shambles. The game'll get cleaned up and you can get back where you belong – on the pitch.'

Dad threw a gentle punch, then sat back wearily.

'I'm in touch with people all around the country. It's much bigger than just the enhancers thing. The clubs, the leagues, the authorities – they've been sucking the life-force from this country for a long time …' He sighed and rubbed the back of his neck. '… far too long. There's a politician, an opposition MP called

Munro Sweet, he's on our side. When we've gathered sufficient evidence, he's going live with it on national TV. In the meantime ...'

Easy felt his father's big hand on his head, ruffling his hair.

'... we all of us have to keep our heads down.'

7
BIG DAY

L ife went on. The new school proved more tedious than Easy could have imagined. He'd never been a particularly high achiever at Highbury High, but here he felt like an intellectual genius. Little or no learning took place in the classrooms: with more than fifty students to every class, it was an uphill struggle for the teachers just to maintain control.

Homework was scant. And with no football to break up the monotony of the days, Easy took to wandering the streets of his new neighbourhood. Week after week, he skirted around pavement kickabouts, head down, walking on by. Since the talk with his father, he avoided the streets around the college where he'd played the rooftop game with Jordan and the boys.

The full implications of what Dad had told him were still sinking in. There were no safe enhancers. Enhancers could *kill*. If he turned pro he would be putting his life at risk. And Gunman Reds had a contract for him to play. The very thing he had looked forward to all these years, he now had to avoid. Joining Gunman Reds could mean *death*.

The new school term and new football season were well under way. Jordan would no longer be out there. No more rooftop matches for Jordan, no more running the streets. Whichever club he'd finally chosen, he'd be away by now, training with other young hopefuls, all of them eager for a place in the squad.

And, despite all Dad had told him, when he thought of Jordan, preparing to make his debut as a pro, Easy couldn't help feeling a pang of envy. Even if all the stuff about enhancers proved to be true, pro soccer – the British Premier League, the FA Cup, and the Corporates League – was *the* most exciting sport to be part of. No two ways about it. And, if the game got cleaned up again, it was where he intended to be.

'*Come on, the Black and Whites ...*'
   '*Up the Reds!*'
Sporadic bouts of excited shouting fluttered and died beneath the enormous wall of sound, pumped overhead from multiple hidden speakers. Every face was turned towards the giant curved screens. Gunman Reds versus arch-rivals New Spurs United, simultaneous and live from Highbury stadium. Each screen showed a different viewpoint – cutting between pitch-side camera, overhead crane, bird's eye airship, player-point-of-view, and back again.

Across the vast hall, Easy and Trix watched from one of the lower galleries.

As one screen showed replays or statistics – ball

speeds, heart-rates of players, shots on goal, corners, fouls and constantly changing betting odds – the other maintained real-time. Punctuated by the thunderous roar of the Highbury crowd, disembodied voices – the commentators, and the players and managers on their personal communicators – boomed above the bars and betting stations.

The whistle blew.

'*O-o-o-oh!*' Highbury's gasp was echoed round the hall by the thousands gazing up at the screens. 'Akashi is down. That looked *nasty*.' The commentator's voice growled. 'The referee is pointing to the spot … *Yes!* … with only ten minutes to go, it's a *penalty!*'

This time the roar from the floor and galleries was deafening – momentarily drowning out all sound from Highbury. Easy and Trix exchanged smiles. The majority of the drinkers and gamblers were clearly Gunners, or at least punters who were by now backing the Reds.

On the left-hand screen, medics dashed to attend Akashi. Gunman's Japanese midfielder still clutched his knee and writhed on the turf, the agony didn't look like an act. The right-hand screen showed angry New Spurs players besieging the referee. Statistics flashed up: the number of offences given against each player. The referee spoke into his mouthpiece, his voice cut loud and clear from invisible speakers. 'Referee request: instant replay of incident.' On screen, players, referee and stadium crowd turned to watch Highbury's own giant screen as it prepared to replay the incident.

Easy chewed a nail. Above the hushed floor, the incident replayed in sync with the replay at the stadium. From Highbury, and from the floor and galleries, jubilant cries of *'Foul!'* rose up to drown the commentators' voices. *'Yes! – Penalty!'*

Week after week, Gunman Reds had been climbing their way towards the top of the table. Now they were neck-and-neck with Blue City Rangers and New Spurs United. It was still early days, scarcely a quarter of the way into the season, but the three teams were already pulling clear from the rest of the pack. Victory today could count for a lot.

Trix held up crossed fingers. 'Here we go!'

Easy nodded and chewed his nail some more. Only a few weeks ago, he had scarcely been aware that a place such as this existed. With Dad out of work, *Highbury@Home*, the Gunman Reds' pay-per-view channel, had been something they could no longer afford. He'd been forced to look for other ways to watch his team. To begin with he'd taken to crouching by the window in his bedroom, watching the screens of neighbours across the street.

Unfortunately, with the high cost of live pay-per-view and the low level of local incomes, people cut the expense of *Highbury@Home* by getting in as many friends and neighbours as would pay. So apartments got very full. And, though the screens were large and close enough for him to follow with Dad's binoculars, his view was often obscured by the sheer number of people shouting, crowding and waving in front of them.

There was another major drawback: watching from his bedroom he got no sound. And if you couldn't hear, the thrill just wasn't the same. A couple of times he'd tried to gain entrance to one of these Gunman supporters' gatherings, but on both occasions the charge to get in had been way beyond his means.

Trix of all people had come up with the solution. She had made new friends more easily than either he or Deena. One of the new friends had told her about Leisure Palaces – so it was sort of her idea. The great thing about Leisure Palaces was: no entrance fee. They made their profits from adults drinking and gambling.

How to get in – that had been the problem. These massive places generally had only one point of entry: past Security at the front door. Big signs outside every Leisure Palace announced *No Unaccompanied Minors*. Trix's idea had been simple – loiter round the corner waiting for the right family group, tag along behind, mingle and – *presto!* – you're through the doors and in.

Once he'd found the bottle to try, it had worked every time. Apart from the few games he'd missed at the start of the season, he'd watched every Gunman match, home and away, live and in glorious surround-sound-and-vision. It hadn't been so easy for Trix to get to all of them – Mum was more restrictive about what hours she allowed her out, supervised or otherwise. But as today was a special occasion, and there'd been an early kick-off, they were watching it together.

'Akashi, at last being stretchered off the field there … a confirmed broken ankle. The crowd here in the

54

stadium standing, heads bowed, as a mark of respect. Such a marvellous young talent … an absolute tragedy.' The commentator's voice disappeared under yet another Highbury roar.

Again the sound echoed round the massive Leisure Palace audience. Easy felt his spine tingle. Such a powerful noise! The tiny hairs on his forearm stood on end.

'It's going to be Ajax Morayne!' boomed the commentator. 'Ajax Morayne – until recently ball-speed world-record-holder for that free-kick against Rangers at the start of the season.'

'Go on, Ajax!' Shaking a fist, Easy yelled at the screen. 'REVENGE! Give us that goal!'

Next to him, Trix cupped her hands round her mouth. 'And while you're at it,' she yelled, 'how about a new world record!'

Ajax Morayne walked calmly over to the spot. As he bent to place the ball, he glanced up towards the New Spurs goalie. The keeper stared back, eyes narrowed. On-screen, and in the giant hall, crowd noise died. The Leisure Palace screens switched to the striker's point-of-view and the goalie's. A mischievous grin slowly spread across Ajax's face. New Spurs' goalie remained stony. Ajax winked. Gunman supporters responded with a cheer. He began backwards pacing, measuring for his run at the ball.

Once again the Gunman Reds' supporters at Highbury and inside the Leisure Palace fell silent. But in the high-banked stands behind the goal, the New

Spurs supporters whistled, booed and roared defiance. A short sharp blast on the whistle. Ajax raised his head, took a deep breath and began the charge. As he accelerated, the New Spurs cacophony rose to a furious crescendo. The keeper reached to his left. Ajax's leg rose, the ball flashed through the air, the net jerked; the goalie was still floating towards the post as Gunman supporters began to cheer.

'How many's that?' Easy panted.

'Ten, I think.' Trix clutched at the rail. 'Only two more to go!'

Easy and Trix staggered and laughed their way up another flight of stairs. Both lifts serving the block were, once again, out of order, but the prospect of climbing twelve flights of stairs hadn't daunted either of them. Their spirits were higher than kites. Ajax Morayne had set a new ball-speed record and, for the first time in the season, Gunman Reds had taken top position in the table.

'Yes!' Easy punched the air as he reached the landing of the twelfth floor, several steps ahead of his gasping sister. 'What a birthday treat!'

Trix collapsed on the floor behind him, clutching her chest and frowning. She lay there watching him till she'd recovered enough to speak. 'The lifts don't have to be out of order for you to run up the stairs, you know, Ease.'

Easy tutted. 'I meant the match, not the running up the stairs, stupid.'

'Oh, in that case, I'm with you. Yeah – what a treat!'

The door to their apartment opened. Stepping out, Mum pulled the door to. She looked anxious. 'Gunman must have won, judging by the smiles on your faces.'

'3–2!' Easy scrambled to his feet.

'*Wem-ber-leeee, Wem-ber-leeee!*' chorused Trix behind him.

'Easy …' Mum's voice stiffened. '… there's somebody here to see you.'

'Dad? Is he back?'

Mum shook her head. 'He should be, but – no.'

'A surprise birthday guest, then?'

'In a manner of speaking …' The frown deepened. '… it's somebody from Gunman Reds – an agent from the youth squad. He says he's come to collect you. You're due to start training tomorrow.'

8

GUNMAN REDS

The journey to Gunman Reds' Nuvillage Training Camp had been incredible. Stretched out on plush burgundy leather, behind darkened windows, he had swept north through London's streets in a purring limousine. They had even passed close to Highbury, heading out to where spaces between buildings grew wider and the countryside began to encroach.

Then on to the fast track: lights twinkling in the dusk, streaking out towards the wilderness, buildings getting thinner on the ground. And after just a few minutes, there it was – the Nuvillage complex, laid out in the darkness at the end of a slip road, floodlit like a space city. Designed by the same mind as Highbury, you could tell straight away.

It looked equally impressive by day. Easy leant against the window frame, letting his gaze glaze over. *How had they located him?* After all Dad's efforts ... The question had kept him awake most of the night, and now, more than twelve hours after he'd said goodbye to Mum and Trix and left with the club officials, it was still buzzing round his head.

What had happened to Dad? Dad had promised he'd be home for his birthday. After everything they'd talked about, it was hard to imagine he'd had a change of heart and told the club officials where to find his son. *Perhaps the club had sent their agents to search him out? Maybe someone had spotted him up on the rooftop, after all?*

'Ready ta go, aye?'

Easy turned from the window. The boy who an hour ago had delivered breakfast on a tray now stood in the open doorway. His fierce-looking eyebrows lifted for emphasis.

'Just about.' Glancing round the room, Easy hurried to the bed and began straightening the covers.

The boy wagged a finger. 'No need ta bother. The bed'll be stripped. You'll no be sleeping here again tonight.'

The duvet dropped from Easy's fingers. 'No?'

The boy shook his head. 'This here's reception quarters – just for the new fellas.' He gestured. 'Come on, pal …'

Easy followed along the corridor.

'I've ta take yi ta see the boss.' The boy gave a low chuckle. 'There'll be nae more lie-ins for *you*. Tonight it's the dorms, same as the rest of us.'

The men were dressed in almost identical training suits: Gunman Red colours and insignia. Across the front of one, emblazoned in large blocky letters, were the words: 'YOUTH COACH' and across the other: 'ASSISTANT YOUTH COACH'.

As Easy entered the room, each man stood.

Completely bald and considerably fatter than his Assistant, the Youth Coach smiled and pumped Easy's hand. 'I'm Sergeant. Welcome to Nuvillage. Please ...' He gestured. '... take a seat.'

In comparison, the Assistant Coach appeared almost skinny. 'Graves,' he said, offering a hand.

Easy shook it and sat.

Settling back in their chairs, the two men studied him. Graves turned to a desktop console. 'Promising reports of your development up until last year ...' He glanced up. '... nothing thereafter. All reports filed by chief scout, Todd Linker ...' The eyes narrowed. 'Your father, apparently, is no longer with us ...'

Easy's heart skipped a beat. 'No longer with us?' he gulped. 'How d'you mean?'

'I believe he took early retirement ...' Sergeant frowned. '... from the club.'

'Oh, yeah ...' Easy swallowed. 'Still very much a supporter, though.'

Sergeant raised an eyebrow. 'He'll be delighted that we've taken up your contract, then?'

Easy nodded. 'Totally.'

'Good.'

'Every boy starts *on probation*.' Graves spread open his arms. 'Medicals, training, match practice, gymnasium and pool work ... when we've seen enough, you'll either be accepted into the fold ...' He embraced thin air. '... or allowed to leave.'

Easy nodded.

'Just remember ...' Sergeant sat back in his chair.

'You belong to us now. To the club. When you're making big money, all sorts of possibilities open up to you, but right now you are *ours*. We've made a down-payment on your future and if we don't think you're doing enough to measure up, *we will make your life hell.*'

The medical had been thorough – more than an hour's worth of tests. The training had been much longer. And, despite his trying to play down his fitness, it had been *exhausting*. Given that he hadn't played or trained for so many weeks, it was amazing he was still on his feet. But – *boy!* – did he *ache*! From the muscles in his neck right down to the Achilles tendon in each ankle, there wasn't a ligament that didn't hurt. Most were silently *screaming*.

Easy slumped on the grass beside the fierce-eyebrowed Scot, his shadow since breakfast. Gently massaging a hamstring, he watched the Assistant Coach jog over.

'Thank you, Robertson.' Graves nodded to the boy. 'Across to pitch five, now.'

Fierce-eyebrows jumped to his feet and sped away.

'OK, young Linker.' Graves beckoned. 'Let's take a look at you in action.'

Rubbing life into his thighs, Easy dragged his body upright, then hobbled off in pursuit. Graves jogged along past two pitches. At the third he stopped. Easy caught up, panting. A hamstring spasmed. He winced.

Graves grinned. 'Feeling it a bit, eh? Most of the

boys find it tough-going the first few days. You'll soon pick up.' Turning to the pitch, he whistled a high piercing note. '*Lads!*' And again. 'Rest up for a minute, lads. Over here.' He gestured. 'Take five.'

The players gathered, red shirts and turquoise ones.

'This is Easy Linker – a new probationer. I want to try him out in different positions. So, I'll be moving you all around from time to time.'

'Look who it is!'

The voice was familiar. Easy turned. He did a double-take. Fez!

'You boys know each other?' Graves glanced from one to the other.

'In a manner of speaking.' Fez sneered. 'We had a couple of kickabouts once upon a time. Thinks he's God's gift, this one.'

Easy groaned inwardly. Talk about pot calling the kettle black!

Graves rubbed his hands gleefully. 'Time for us to find out. Go easy on him, lads. Remember what your first day was like. He's been training with Sergeant for three hours, he's … not at his best.' He turned to Easy. 'I'd like to start you in midfield.' He smiled. 'Let's put you in a turquoise shirt – opposite your friend. There's a kit bag behind the goal. Soon as you're changed, come and join in.'

Easy jogged up to the edge of the box. What was he doing – he wasn't supposed to be playing well or even close to it, but the last few minutes he'd been forgetting himself. He'd delivered two beautiful passes and then, when the captain had gone and lost it, he'd retrieved it for him.

These boys were slick and fast. Unbelievably fast – he'd given up trying to race them a long time ago. But that had made the urge to outplay them all the stronger – and that was what he had to resist. The skills had to be kept under wraps. Nuvillage was what Dad had been trying to protect him from, and now he was here. This was where it all started.

New recruits were probably put on enhancers as soon as they began training. He would have to keep his wits about him. Dad had said they were killers.

'Mate!' The ball was in play and coming his way. Time to do a foolish thing. Easy ran to meet it, brought it down controlled. Nice. It was so hard not to.

'On the wing!'

Easy measured the opposition, the layout of the two teams. Took off, dribbling, head down. Ahead of him, around the goal-mouth, players jostled. To the right, on the wing, the fast boy with the long legs and arms was waving and dodging behind his marker.

Two red shirts shuffled forward to meet him, one shadowing the other. The front one lunged. Easy dodged left, skipped the outstretched leg and pushed on. Number two side-stepped into his path, hunkering down, eye on the ball. Easy danced the ball back and forth, edging forward. The boy glanced up, Easy twisted left, jerked right and slipped the ball through his legs. Collecting round the back, he made a bee-line for the goal. Too easy.

'Pass it!'

'Come on, pass it out!'

Reds were on his tail and there were four or five turquoise shirts in the box, dodging between the defenders. The two strikers had thrown themselves into open space ready to receive a pass. The one nearest the right post had a perfect line on open goal, he couldn't miss, he was waving his hand, signalling wildly …

Easy kept on going, weaving towards the posts.

'Man on!'

Another red lunged. Easy swerved. The stray foot caught his ankle and threw his balance. He staggered, regained momentum and powered on past two of his teammates. Two more Reds blocked his path, behind them there was only the goalie and that turquoise striker. Easy barged straight through the middle, shouldering defenders out of his way. Again the stray boot – this time hacking at his shins. Thank God for the pads. Arms flailing, he ploughed over and on.

He was in the clear zone. Over to his right the striker gestured again. 'Come on!' The tall boy who had scored the last two goals, now itching for his hat-trick. Crouched midway between the posts, the goalie darted his eyes from one adversary to the other. Easy slowed a little, dummied the pass, then accelerated straight at the goalie. He skipped, *whacked* it with all his might and tumbled, sprawling head-first into the net.

'No!'

'Idiot!'

'How can anyone miss from point-blank range!'

'And it was a metre over the crossbar – what a blockhead!'

Face down on the ground, Easy smiled to himself. *A metre over* – right where he'd wanted it! He struggled to his feet.

'Ever hear of passing?' Angry teammates gathered, muttering and cussing under their breath. 'Should have got rid of it, you bimbo.' 'Totally useless!' 'You had all the time in the world. What were you trying to prove?' The red-shirts looked on, amused.

Graves, in his Assistant Coach jersey, jogged up behind a bemused-looking Fez. He scowled at Easy. 'Half your team were hanging around the goal-mouth. Did you think you were the only one playing?'

'Sorry …' In each boy's eyes, Easy saw sneering contempt. He shuddered. Nobody liked a selfish player, especially an incompetent one. It was a horrible feeling. 'I just forgot where I was.' He held up his hands. 'Sorry. It was a heat-of-the-moment thing.'

'Believe that and you'll believe anything.'

Heads turned. A group of boys had gathered behind the goal-line – they too were wearing red or turquoise shirts, though the designs were different. Others in the same shirts were making their way towards the gymnasium.

'That boy's never been any different.'

The voice was familiar. Easy squinted at the group, his eyes focused on a freckled grin. The grin was unmistakable – *Jordan!*

2
GYM

Strapped into the padded seat, Easy took hold of the rubber grips, one in each hand. Snatching a deep breath, he braced his strength against the hinged bar and pushed. Slowly, the stack of iron blocks rose beside him. As his arms reached full extension, he exhaled, locked shoulders, then let the bar begin a gradual descent back to starting position, forcing his muscles to resist all the way down. Then again. And again …

Boys puffed and groaned as they heaved the heavy weights. Some worked on machines, others used free weights: barbells and dumbbells. Muscles strained and bulged around the gym, faces grimaced with exertion. The bench press, the leg press, shoulder press, squats, abdominal crunches, triceps curls and biceps curls – endless sets of repetitions. Everyone training individual body parts.

With a final heave, Easy once more raised the heavy bar. 'Eeeee*argh*!' At its limit, his strength left him and the bar came crashing back to rest.

From the early morning wake-up call to nightly

lights-out in the dorms, every aspect of life at Nuvillage was strictly regimented. Way too strictly for his liking but, as the days went by, he found himself gradually settling into the routine. Except, that was, for the moment when they were supposed to take their supplements and performance-enhancers during breakfast and supper.

Each boy's special requirements were worked out following his initial assessment. The chief dietician had explained the importance of taking the supplements and performance-enhancers and the hazards of failing to do so. Your 'programme' was designed to gradually adapt your body for the rigours it would face in the professional game. Uncontrolled withdrawal could result in extremely unpleasant symptoms as your body struggled to cope without the chemicals it had grown used to.

The tablets were always there at mealtimes, in a small cup, waiting for you at your place setting. None of the tablets were labelled, none of the boys knew what they were taking, but all seemed to swallow without compunction. Apart, that was, from him. From the very first day, he had palmed the pills at each sitting, before slipping them into his pocket for later disposal. He had become quite adept at it. And the master of the faked swallow.

Unstrapping himself from the shoulder-press machine, Easy made his way to one of the bench-pressing stations. Slipping himself under the bars, he lay back and lifted his feet up on to the bench. With a sigh, he let his eyes close.

During the week of his arrival he'd been exhausted, the non-stop daily training had been far more arduous than anything he'd anticipated – a total shock to the system. Every night, the moment his head touched the pillow he'd been asleep: every morning, forcing his body out of bed had been a battle and a half.

His sessions in the gym had been laughable. On one occasion, lying down to bench-press, he'd been so exhausted from all the running around and match practice work, he had actually fallen asleep. Such had been his state of fatigue that first week, there'd been several training machines on which he'd been unable to shift even the lowest weight.

Now, though, things were different. After only a few weeks, strength and stamina appeared to have recovered and were slowly developing. He was less tired and felt fitter and stronger than he could remember. Of course, in the training exercises and in the gym he was still some way behind the other boys, but then he didn't expect to keep up with them – they were taking the tablets and he wasn't. Most of them had already been accepted as full-time trainees. *He* didn't want to be.

It was a gradual adjustment. The muscles were aching less and less and, increasingly, he'd found the mental energy to focus on convincing everyone, coaches and boys alike, that he was an over-ambitious player of mediocre talent.

'Catching up on lost sleep?'

Easy blinked open his eyes. 'Jordan!'

'How come you're still training on your own?'

Pushing aside Easy's legs, Jordan seated himself at the end of the bench.

Easy pulled himself upright. He shrugged. And stared – it was hard not to, Jordan's physique had really transformed since they'd first met in their rooftop encounter. His thigh muscles looked massive, his arms and chest were filling out like a pro's too. The two of them had hardly seen each other since the first day, they hadn't spoken more than a few words. The regime made it practically impossible – they were in different intake groups, they didn't eat together or train together and their dormitories were at opposite ends of the vast living quarters.

'You should try training with a partner,' said Jordan, 'it's much more effective – both of you push each other, you work loads harder.'

'I've not made a lot of friends,' said Easy. 'Too much boasting, not enough skill.'

'Not enough skill!' Jordan chuckled. 'You! I sussed you were up to something when we played that first time. And then when I saw you whacking it miles above the crossbar, I thought: *What's he playing at?*'

Easy shuffled closer. 'You did me a big favour slagging off my playing ability in front of everyone. There's a lot of respect for you round here. When you rubbished me – they all sat up and took notice.'

'Any time.' Jordan grinned. 'My training partner's sick. Why don't we work out together? You'd be doing me a favour.'

'OK.' Easy reached back to select the weight level on the stack. 'I'll go first.' Lying back under the bar, he took hold of the rubber grips and braced himself, ready to push.

'You want to lift your knees up towards your chest,' said Jordan. 'It'll stop you using your leg muscles to help.'

Easy did as instructed.

Crouching down, Jordan reached in behind the bench and raised the level of weight. 'Isolation,' he said. 'It's all about isolating the muscles and pushing them to their limit.'

Easy began to lift the loaded bar. Pushing till his arms were fully extended, he slowly lowered it down again.

'One …' Jordan counted as Easy puffed and laboured. 'Two … Three … Four … Five … Six … Seven – come on! Eight – come *on*! Nine … yes … *Ten! Yes!* Well done! OK, my turn.'

The two boys swapped places. Leaning back, Jordan selected his starter weight.

'Seventy kilos!' Easy stared. 'That's more than double what I've just lifted.'

Jordan grinned up at him from the bench. 'I've been on *the programme* longer than you.' Slowly but with very little apparent effort, he raised the bar till his arms were fully extended. 'So, how come you've changed your mind about Gunman Reds? The deals are unbeatable. Even *I* signed up, for God's sake, and you know who I support. You're supposed to be a Gunman through and through.' The weight bar came slowly down.

Up down, up down, even and controlled. 'Four …

Five … Six …' Easy counted aloud the repetitions, till Jordan reached his fifteenth.

Jordan's face was straining. The weights crashed down. His chest heaved. 'I hear you're up in front of the panel this afternoon,' he panted, sliding out from under the bar. 'You're probably the best young player in Nuvillage – how come you want to fail your assessment?' Stripping off his shirt, he flexed his chest muscles. 'Think you can get a better offer somewhere else?'

Easy shook his head.

'Why then?'

'Enhancers …' Easy's voice trailed off as two older boys took up positions at a neighbouring machine. 'It's not safe to talk here … could we meet up later?'

'OK.' Jordan nodded. 'Ten before lights-out. Last cubicle on the left, C-wing latrine.'

There were three people sitting behind the table alongside Sergeant and Graves, two of them Easy recognized. The doctor who had examined him when he first arrived had examined him again only twenty-four hours ago. And the enormous weights instructor from the gym. In the middle, a smartly dressed woman sat studying some documents. She glanced up as Easy scraped back the chair and seated himself. Cold and critical eyes, thin painted lips, and a rigidity to the face, as if every feature were set in stone.

Sergeant made a coughing sound as if preparing to speak. But the smartly dressed woman beat him to it. 'Carnegie Randal.' The accent was American. 'I'm based here and at Highbury, working for Gunman's Special Operations. I report directly to The Board. The other people here ...' She gestured. 'I believe you know?'

Easy nodded.

'And you are Easy Linker, son of Todd Linker who, till recently, was chief talent-scout at Highbury.' Randal peered straight into Easy's eyes. Searching. 'I'll come straight to the point. Mr Sergeant and his team here have been studying you over the past few weeks. They are unhappy with your performance. In training and on the field you have proved to be far from satisfactory. Have you anything to say for yourself?'

This was encouraging! Easy frowned and pinched the bridge of his nose. Time for some acting. 'Personally,' he said, 'I don't think that's fair. Not once since I arrived have I been given a true crack of the whip. I've been forced to play in midfield, when it's clear my talents lie elsewhere.'

'I've viewed footage of you in action,' said Randal. 'Where would you say you play best?'

'Up front, obviously.'

'What about the rest of the field?'

'Yeah, I'm pretty much all right all over, but ...'

'... you keep hogging the ball? Tripping over your own feet? Missing your shots on goal? It's as if ...' Randal's voice hardened its edge. '... as if you were *trying* to play like an incompetent.' The eyes were steel. Round the edges they softened a touch. 'Mr Sergeant here claims there have been moments on the pitch when you have demonstrated flashes of ... brilliance. He believes that you are an exceptionally talented player pretending to be otherwise. Now, why would you want to do that?' Clasping her hands, she leant across the desk. 'That's what we'd all like to know.'

Easy glanced from face to face. Sergeant and Graves had sussed what he was up to, they'd suspected all along. What about the others? All of them must have been watching him like a hawk. He frowned and shrugged. 'I don't understand what you're on about.'

Randal shot him a look. 'Apparently you've not been swallowing your tablets.' She tapped the sheets of paper on the desk in front of her. 'Seem to have made a bit of a habit of it, too. Bit silly ...' The patronizing tone was almost friendly, caring. 'So, why aren't you taking your supplements and enhancers then? Don't you want to be a pro?'

Randal's smile had an almost maternal warmth. Easy sensed danger. 'Of course I do. I've always dreamed of playing for Gunman Reds. It's just ...' He groped for a convincing reason. 'I have a bit of a problem with taking tablets – I'm one of those people that *can't*. I gag. I know it's pathetic ...' He lowered his eyes. 'I was embarrassed to tell anyone. I thought – a place like this, everybody's going to laugh at me if I come straight out and admit it. So I had to pretend.' He was blushing, he could feel his ears burning. *Would they believe him?* 'I flushed them down the toilet.'

73

Randal frowned.

Easy chewed the inside of his lip, waiting for an outburst.

But Randal simply tutted. 'What a silly boy. You should have come and told someone.' Her voice was practically sing-song. She smiled and gently shook her head. 'It doesn't matter: this infringement was picked up on the first day, so no harm's done. All the supplements and enhancers you should have been getting were added to your food. The tablets were empty placebos.'

Easy was speechless.

'Your training continues tomorrow,' said Sergeant.

'If you were hoping we would reject you ...' Randal shook her head. 'Forget it.'

10
SNEAKING

In the hour before lights-out, monitors patrolled to ensure that noise and activity were kept to an acceptable level and that boys remained in their allotted dorms. The monitors were generally *squaddies* – older boys who had progressed through the initial training regime and been accepted into one of the squads. If one of them made a report against you, it meant being put on a week's cleaning duty as a punishment and given extra hard training sessions when everyone else was relaxing before dinner.

In addition to the squaddies, a few youth trainees who liked to throw their weight about had been co-opted to the job. Fez was one such, and every evening when the rest of them were sitting around on their bunks watching football, reading, chatting, or playing cards and having a laugh he patrolled the corridors of D-wing.

Easy crept along the hushed corridor. The sound of boys laughing in the dorm was all but muffled by sound-proofed walls and doors. Getting past Fez wasn't going to take a great deal of skill – he was usually to be found loitering at the end of a corridor, sucking up to whichever squaddie he happened to bump into. The sound of his distinctive nasal tones drifted along the corridor. Easy padded his way as far as the stairs, then cocked an ear.

'... the guy's a legend in his own lifetime.'

'What I wouldn't give to be in his boots.' A squaddie's voice, not one Easy recognized.

'By the sound of things,' said Fez, 'your chances might have edged a little closer tonight.'

'Nah!' said the squaddie. 'It'll just be some small problem. He'll be right as rain in a few days' time. It's probably just too many games, too close together. The pressure up at their level is really tough.'

Fez concurred with a grunt.

Slowly, silently, Easy tiptoed up the stairs away from the voices. Two floors above, he slipped into C-wing corridor and, treading stealthily, made his way along to the latrine.

The door closed behind him. The place was empty, or at least it appeared to be: no one brushing their teeth, nobody having a wash or taking a leak. Perhaps the boys on C-wing were already tucked up in bed! Crouching down, Easy made his way between the toilet cubicles, peering beneath the doors, checking for feet. At the furthest cubicle on the left he pushed against the door.

'*Oi!* D'you mind!' Seated on the toilet, shorts around his ankles, Jordan looked up from his magazine and grinned. 'So how did it go with the assessment panel?'

Easy grimaced and shook his head.

'That good, huh? They sussed your little scam?'

Easy shrugged. 'They spotted I wasn't taking my enhancers.'

'You sound surprised,' said Jordan. 'They're not stupid, you know.'

'They've been slipping them into my food,' said Easy. 'At least – so they say. They warned me against trying to leave. They said I'd get serious withdrawal coming off the stuff too suddenly. They said it could kill me.'

Jordan nodded. 'Par for the course if you're not weaned off ultra-slowly. I hear that's down to the other filth they give you, as much as the enhancers. But that's the deal, whichever club you play for. Once you're on a programme, they've got you by the short and curlies. Very hard if you want to jump ship.' He chuckled. 'That's why *when you play with a club, you stay with a club.*'

'I don't believe them,' said Easy. 'I certainly don't *feel* enhanced. They must be bluffing.'

Jordan reached up and squeezed Easy's biceps. He grinned. 'Can't say you do feel enhanced, but then: it can take a while for the effects to kick in. Do you still plan to leave?'

Easy shrugged. 'Dunno.' After the assessment panel, he needed to think.

Jordan yanked up his shorts. 'So how come you took so long getting here?'

'On our wing, the monitors actually patrol and keep a look-out. C-wing seems to be asleep.'

'I don't know about this C-wing lot.' Jordan glanced at his watch. 'But right now, everyone on A-wing'll be watching the footie highlights.'

Easy nodded. 'A couple of the monitors were chatting in the stairwell just now. Someone got injured, by the sound of things it's one of the big names.'

Jordan gripped Easy's arm. 'That must've been who I saw ... I had to go out on a balcony, it was the only way to get round our monitors. But as I was climbing back in through a window, I caught this private ambulance-car come whizzing in through the gates.'

'You think they've brought whoever it was *here*, to the medical block?'

'Definitely.' Jordan nodded. 'They take them up to the second floor – high security and all that, you must have noticed when you were over there?'

Easy nodded. 'Yeah ... I wondered what that was all about – the elevator goes straight from the first floor to the third, doesn't it? It never stops at the second. *Access Restricted* the button said. There was a slot for some kind of security key.'

'Yeah. It's all top secret. And there's a locked and guarded staircase round the back. I've been dying to take a look.'

'Are you serious?'

'Course I am!' Jordan jumped to his feet. '*All work and no play* ... we've got to have some fun and adventure once in a blue moon. Don't tell me you're chicken?'

'No!' Easy puffed out his chest. 'Course not!'

'Come on, then!' Clambering up on the toilet seat, Jordan braced his legs against the cubicle walls, reached up and pushed against a ceiling ventilation grille. The grille gave easily and lifted out of view.

'Here we go!' With one swift heave, Jordan pulled himself up through the hole and disappeared into the air duct. His head re-emerged. 'This way, ladies and gentlemen! For the Grand Tour of Nuvillage, please follow me!'

Scrambling up behind him, Easy blinked in the scant light. The air duct was cramped but large enough for him to crawl comfortably on hands and knees. A little way up the tunnel, Jordan waited for him to replace the ceiling panel. The light grew even dimmer.

'These ducts carry sound,' whispered Jordan, 'so I suggest we crawl quietly.'

'Have you done this before?' said Easy.

Jordan grinned. 'Evenings get awful dull round here when there's no footie to watch.'

With Jordan blocking off any possibility of light from the front and no light reaching him from behind, Easy found himself crawling in almost total darkness.

Every so often Jordan would whisper a warning about a shaft or a ceiling grille. Shafts were scary vertical drops that just opened up in the middle of the duct; usually, though not always, at a place where ducts joined or crossed. The shafts went down to the basement and up to the roof. Enormous extractor fans sucked out stale air and blew in fresh.

Peering down through the grilles was not quite so terrifying. In fact, when there was someone below, it gave Easy a small thrill to be watching unobserved. Slowly but surely, they were progressing in the right direction.

Easy's head hit something hard.

'Oi, careful!' whispered Jordan. 'That's my rear!'

'Sorry. Didn't see it.'

'It's big enough,' said Jordan.

'You should get lights,' said Easy.

The two boys chuckled in the dark.

'There's another shaft here,' said Jordan. 'We're in the right area, but on the wrong floor. We need to go down a level.'

Easy nodded. 'How do we do that?'

'The shafts, of course.'

'The shafts! But – we've got no ropes or anything.'

'Ropes shmopes!' Jordan snorted. 'Feet are all we need. I've done it loads of times before. You'll see.'

Easy felt distinctly uneasy. His stomach was tightening, soon it would be tying itself in knots.

In the scant light Easy could just make out Jordan removing his trainers and tying them round his neck. He followed suit. The metal felt cold against his soles.

'Bare feet,' whispered Jordan. 'They stick against this stuff beautifully.' He lowered himself into the shaft, then lifted his hands.

Easy's heart skipped a beat.

'Your bum and one foot press back,' said Jordan. 'The other foot braces forward. And *presto!* – solid as a rock. Using your hands against the sides, you can release your feet and move them lower.'

'Yeah?'

'Yeah. Honest – it's easy. I'll go first to show you.' Jordan gave a low chuckle in the dark. 'That way, if you drop, I'll be there below to break your fall.'

'Thanks!'

It wasn't so bad, if you forgot about the height and the danger of what you were doing. Shift by shift, Easy grew more confident that the business of pressing feet against shaft worked just as well as Jordan had said. And, with the darkness, he couldn't see a thing, not even Jordan's head below him; that made things easier – he could pretend that what he was doing was really quite safe.

'OK ...' Jordan's whisper floated up. 'Second-floor ducts coming up. Our stop.'

Glancing down between his legs, Easy saw Jordan's silhouette disappearing into the horizontal duct. His heart began to race. There was *nothing* now between him and the basement, *three floors down*. Bracing the shaft walls with his hands, he shifted his body weight downwards. The muscles in his legs began to shake. 'Oh *God* ...'

'Nearly there, mate,' urged Jordan. 'Less than a metre to go, just one more shift. Then all you've got to do is get your feet on the two ducts, crouch down and, Bob's your uncle, you're in!'

Bracing his hands against the cold metal, Easy began sliding his feet downwards. His hands were sweating ... they were starting to slide ... 'Where's the ledge?' There was panic in his voice. 'Where *is* it?'

'Just a little further, come on.' Jordan's voice was calm, reassuring.

Easy felt a hand touch his foot in the darkness, gently guiding it down to the edge of the duct. As his other foot found its own way, he struggled to control his breathing. 'Thanks ...' he panted, crouching and ducking inside the duct. '... I was starting to lose it!' He flopped on the duct floor, his heart beating like a drum.

Jordan chuckled. 'You did fine. That was just first time nerves.'

'First time?' Easy felt his heart race again. 'I don't *ever* want to do that again!'

'Then you'd better hope there's another way out.'

Keeping track of time and direction was hard when you were crawling through darkness disrupted only by light from the occasional ventilation grille. Each grille revealed a new glimpse of the medical block's secret second floor – most of the rooms appeared to contain laboratory equipment and computers. There was some *serious* research going on. More surprising, and certainly more alarming, were the guards patrolling every corridor. Their hip-holsters carried large batons and *guns*.

'*Aaaaaaaagh! Aaagh-aagh!*'

Easy shivered. 'What's that?' Hairs on the back of his neck prickled.

The faint cries echoed along the air duct. '*Aaaagh-aaaaaaagh!*'

'Sounds like someone in a lot of pain,' said Jordan.

'It sounds near by,' said Easy. 'Let's keep moving.'

The two boys hurried along the duct on their hands and knees, the agonized cries growing louder and more racked as they advanced. Then, quite suddenly, they changed to the sound of sobbing. And there were other voices too.

Illuminated by the light from another ventilation grille, Jordan turned and put a finger to his lips. 'This is the one.'

Easy lowered his face to the grille and peered through the slats. *'Oh my God …!'*

There, laid out below, staring wild-eyed up at the grille, was Ajax Morayne.

11

TRUTH

'*Aaaagh-aaaaah-aaaaaaaaagh!* No-no-no-no-*aaagh!*'
Ajax Morayne thrashed and writhed. His wild,
violent movements shook the massive recliner he
was strapped to. 'I never ... I never ... I *promise* ... I
never ...' He grunted, panted, gasped. Over and over
his body jerked.

Men and women, dressed in medical coats,
shouted instructions at one another. While some
attempted to connect monitoring equipment to his
body, or keep in place drips, wires and tubes, others
tried physically to restrain his movement. One of the
women kept bending close to Morayne's ear. Her
words were swallowed by the din as Morayne
continued to thrash and writhe.

Easy glanced across at Jordan.

The stripy light from the grille, gave Jordan's
shocked expression a spookier cast. 'What are they
doing to the poor guy?' he hissed. 'Torturing him?'

'*Aaaagh!* No! *Please*, no! No-no-no-no-no-*aaaaagh!*'
Morayne's back suddenly arched; his whole body
rose, straining against the straps, tensing as if an

84

electric current had been passed from head to toe, contracting every muscle fibre. His jaw was tightly clenched; saliva bubbled at his lips. He spluttered and gurgled through his teeth; it sounded as if his own throat were constricting itself and choking him. 'Please!' He gasped. 'Please!'

Again, the woman bent to his ear. 'You must tell us.' She was practically shouting this time, to make herself heard over Morayne's grunting and groaning. 'Tell us what we need to know, and I can give you the medication to make this go away.'

'I didn't ...' Morayne's body spasmed. 'I didn't ...' He tried again, forcing the words out through still-clenched teeth. '... didn't make any mistakes ...'

'You must have,' said the woman in the white coat. Her voice was soft and gentle, as though she were reprimanding a naughty toddler. 'Otherwise you wouldn't be suffering like this, would you, young man?'

'Didn't!' blurted Morayne. 'Took them all ...' His breathing came in quick gasps. '... at the right times ... as directed.' He spasmed again. '*Aaaaaaaagh!*'

'OK ...' The woman gave a little shrug of resignation. 'We should be able to check your story when we complete our tests, Mr Morayne. Thank you for your co-operation.' She nodded to one of her colleagues, a balding man with a neat beard. He pressed a small implement against Morayne's abdomen. 'You can rest now,' said the woman. Her colleague pressed a button.

One final spasm. Morayne twitched. His body went limp.

'Jeeeezus!' hissed Jordan. 'They just killed –'

'*Shhhh!*' Easy put a finger to his lips. 'Listen …'

'Monitor tetra-penhaldadrine and sarbubitol levels …' The woman in the white coat spoke to the man with the neat beard. 'Hook him up to the drip. Keep an eye on adrenal and neuronal activity. When both have stabilized, you can start administering the recovery programme.'

The man nodded obediently.

'Dr Singh,' said the woman, 'Dr Maxwell, Dr Gruber …' Three of the men in white coats separated from the other medics administering to Morayne. They gathered round her. 'What do we think, gentlemen?'

The man wearing a turban shook his head. 'Same pattern, same symptoms. It doesn't look good.'

The shorter, bespectacled man shrugged. 'We know what we'll find …'

'What do they expect!' snapped the third man. 'Cutting corners, cutting corners all the time. If you introduce these substances without long-term trials you're bound to discover side-effects that weren't predicted. Everyone knows that.' He huffed. 'But what do *they* care for the health and well-being of players?'

The woman nodded and sighed. 'I guess it's back to tests again. Perhaps we can come up with something.' She turned. 'I have to report to Randal. I'll be back as soon as I can.'

Jordan's eyes met Easy's across the grille. His lips mouthed the question. *Enhancers?*

Easy nodded.

'You knew about this?' whispered Jordan. 'Is that why you played badly?'

'I found out a few weeks before my birthday.'

Jordan leant closer. 'How?'

Easy swallowed. 'My dad.'

'What's up? Cramp?'

Biting his lip, Easy nodded. It *hurt*. He wanted to scream and yell.

'Too long in one position.'

Easy had already stretched out his leg and flexed his toes. Groping for his foot in the dark, he rubbed and squeezed it. Relief took its time.

'What d'you reckon?' said Jordan. 'Give it another few minutes?'

It was gone midnight. Apart from the occasional guard still patrolling in the corridors, only the woman in the white coat remained. The rest of her colleagues had left some time ago, but she had sat in her laboratory office, working at the computer, for ages. Then, a little while ago, she had put her computer to sleep and wandered through to the next room, to keep watch over the unconscious Morayne.

Scrambling along the duct, Easy and Jordan had watched her through the ventilation grilles. After a while, she had settled herself in a chair under a blanket and closed her eyes. A guard on his rounds had popped his head round the door and bade her goodnight, only to be greeted by gentle snoring sounds. She was fast asleep.

'OK.' Easy stretched out his leg and flexed his foot again. The cramp was definitely receding. 'She might be a light sleeper. A few more minutes just to be on the safe side.' He glanced across at his friend. 'You don't have to do this with me, you know. I told you – I can manage on my own.'

Jordan snorted. A smirk twitched on the visible half of his face. 'You might be able to get down there, but can you get back out?'

Easy turned away from the light. He was more than grateful for Jordan's company. He hadn't given practicalities much thought. So much other stuff had been going through his mind. 'All right then.' Giving his leg one last rub, he leant over, lifted the grille and slid it along the duct. 'Let's go.'

Hanging from the ceiling, Easy gently swung, let go and dropped down, knees bent, on to a work-bench. He froze, not even breathing, *listening*. But there was nothing. Sliding to the floor, he grabbed a stool and heaved it up on to the work-bench.

Jordan climbed down. 'Right!' He rubbed his hands together, excitedly. 'Let's get searching. What are we looking for?'

'I'm not sure – reports, correspondence, tests results – anything that shows there might be problems with enhancers.'

'Where do we start – the offices?'

Easy nodded. 'I'll take hers. You take the one next door. We need to get a move on.'

Jordan winked. 'OK, boss.'

The walls of the office were lined with shelves of

files. Scrambling on to the desk, Easy reached up for one of the higher ones. Had to start somewhere. The file was labelled with a series of numbers and contained sheets of more numbers – nothing that meant anything to him. He slotted it back and pulled out another from lower down. Same again. *Waste of time.*

Plonking himself in the swivel chair, he tapped the keyboard to wake the computer. While it was sorting itself out, he turned his attention to the desk's drawers. 'OK ...' he mumbled, ' ... what have we here?' Pens, paper, paperclips, rubber bands, a tube of micro-discs and a set of keys in the top one. Opening the tube, Easy emptied the discs on to the desk. They were the rewritable type with data-sensitive chromo casings – at a glance you could see which ones contained data and approximately how much.

He placed the keys on the desk-top and pulled open the second drawer. Envelopes of various sizes – nothing to write home about. The bottom drawer contained three brown-stained mugs, a jar of coffee, a packet of tea and some biscuits. Pushing the drawers shut, he turned his attention to the screen.

The computer's search program came up with 274 files when Easy asked it to look for any containing the word 'enhancer'. Creating a new folder on the screen desktop, he duplicated the found files into it. He repeated this process with 'Category P' and netted a further 87. Time to shove a micro-disc into the drive.

Hi-Sec micro 5000. Iris and voice scan. The message flashed up across the screen. *Please state your name.*

Easy racked his brain. 'Ajax,' he drawled trying to imitate the accent. 'Ajax Morayne.' The voice wouldn't fool anybody, but to have used his own name would have left them in no doubt. He set the computer copying the files he had gathered. While this was being carried out he typed 'Morayne' into the search program and sent it off looking.

'Nothing doing in that one.' Jordan poked his head round the door. 'Having any luck?'

'Hard to say ...' Easy rattled the keys he'd found. 'They might open an interesting door somewhere.' He nodded towards the screen. 'I'm copying stuff that might be connected. Hey! Now this might be interesting!'

Jordan leant over his shoulder. 'What've you found? "Ajax Morayne." OK! Let's open it.'

'Hang on a minute ...' Easy clicked the mouse. 'Let's take a look at the folder where the search program found it.' He clicked again.

'*Wow* – Dolenz ...' said Jordan.

'And Embolo ...' said Easy

'Huckerby ...'

'Hughes ...'

'Gregory ...'

'Kowalski ...'

'Shapiro ...'

'McNulty ...'

'Ze ...'

The two boys looked at each other. 'Gunman players who've retired from the game with injuries,' said Easy. 'Every single one of them.'

'Yeah,' said Jordan. 'Seeing their names listed like that makes you realize – there's been quite a few over the last two or three years.'

'And all of them left before their time,' said Easy. 'We're *definitely* having these.' Duplicating the files, he dragged them to the mini-disc icon. 'Potential dynamite.'

'I'd love to take a look,' said Jordan.

Easy clicked on the file labelled 'Damon Huckerby.' The screen refilled with a list: dates, names of drugs, quantities administered, effects observed.

'Jeeez!' Jordan slapped the desk. 'Look at that lot – the guy was a walking chemical factory. Let's see if we can find mine.'

'Sorry – no time,' said Easy. 'The guard's due round – we have to get out of here.' As the mini-disc ejected from its slot, he pocketed it and set the computer to sleep. 'Come on!'

He hurried to where the stool was perched on the work-bench. The ceiling looked high. Very high. 'So what's the escape plan?' he hissed, turning to Jordan.

'You have to leave.'

Easy frowned. 'What are you talking about – we both do.'

'No – I mean escape from Nuvillage.' Jordan's face was grave. 'Come on – Morayne looked *badly* sick. If that was the result of enhancers they've been giving him ...' He shook his head. '... that is serious bad news. For *all* of us. Those files you've got on disc could hold the answers. You have to get them out of here.'

'I was planning to.'

Jordan shook his head. 'You have to do it *now*.' Jumping up on the work-bench, he held out his hand to Easy. 'You're the only person who can,' he said, climbing astride the stool. 'Right now, up on the stool with me.'

Easy obeyed.

'OK – count of three …' Jordan grabbed Easy's calves. 'You jump. I'm going to give you a boost. Grab hold of the edge and pull yourself up. One … two … three …'

Easy jumped, the extra power from Jordan's assistance thrust him upwards. But as his hands gripped the edge and he heaved himself up, there was a gasp from below.

'*Whoa* …' With a grunt and a crash, Jordan and the toppled stool hit the floor.

From inside the air duct, Easy heard shouts and footsteps as guards raised the alarm and came running. 'Jordan …' he hissed. 'Jordan, come on, *quick!*'

'Ooch …' Jordan stumbled to his feet, rubbing the back of his neck. 'It's too high.' He shook his head. 'Couldn't do it without a boost.' The grin made it clear: he had known only one of them could get back up. He was *trapped*.

Frantic shouts and footsteps grew louder, guards carrying batons and guns were getting closer. There was movement too in the room next door. Jordan held up a set of keys – the keys from the desk. 'I'm going to try these out,' he whispered. 'Should create some kind of diversion for you. Head back the way we came. No need to go up or down any more shafts, just keep going till you hit the far side of the complex.'

Voices and footsteps were in the corridor.

'You should reach a big slatted air outlet,' hissed Jordan. 'I got down that far before on my wanderings. Here – ' He pulled a key from the ring and chucked it up into the duct. 'When you get there, use this to unscrew it. Should do the trick. All you'll have to do then is *jump*.' The grin was mischievous. 'Quick – close the grille!'

Easy felt suddenly very scared and lost for words. 'You'll … you'll be OK,' he stuttered, 'won't you?'

'Course I will,' said Jordan. 'What's the worst they can do to me?'

Easy didn't like to think. 'When all this is over,' he said, 'you're going to see just how good I really play. I'm the best.'

'You?' Jordan chuckled. 'Don't make me laugh! You may be better than you've been letting on, but you ain't even in my league! *I* am the best.'

'We'll see,' said Easy. 'First to score?'

'No problem.' Jordan winked. 'Loser has to streak?'

'What!'

'Not so confident?' said Jordan.

Voices were outside the door.

'OK,' whispered Easy. 'You're on.'

'Now, push off,' said Jordan. '*Scram!*'

Easy's hand shook as he slid the grille closed.

'Next time we play,' Jordan grinned, 'you'd better pray it's somewhere discreet!'

12

ON THE RUN

Easy blinked open his eyes and shivered. A soft drizzle was tickling his face. His body felt stiff, broken even. He lifted his arm to glance at his watch. 8.17. He'd been waking and glancing like this, every quarter of an hour or so, since first light. Five minutes more and he'd force himself to get up. He clutched himself. Five more minutes ...

It wasn't comfortable. No way was it comfortable, but it was nicer than having to wake up, get up and face the world. *Out there* was something he really didn't want to have to deal with on this dull, damp, grey morning. It didn't help that every single bone in his body ached like it'd been smashed with a ten-kilo sledge-hammer.

Easy reached a hand up to his neck and gently rubbed. *Oh God ... how it ached!* He had put his poor body through something of a rough time in the last thirty-six hours. Crawling, jumping, running, walking, jogging, walking – on the go non-stop in the pouring rain. Pushing himself to keep going.

He had hitched a ride into London, but only as far

as the outskirts, so then he had walked and walked and walked some more ... And when he'd finally found a place to snatch some rest, he'd been forced to make his bed on cold, hard concrete. No wonder he felt so bad.

It was time to get up. Slowly, very slowly, Easy tipped himself over on to his side and shook off the damp old cardboard and newspapers he'd been using as covers. Rolling himself on to his feet, he gently straightened up; the joints felt tight, and the muscles ached from their exertions. He checked his pocket for the micro-disc.

The street outside was Trix's route to school – that was why he'd picked the place. Through the holes in corrugated sheeting he could watch without being noticed. In the dismal light of day it didn't seem such an excellent choice: scant shelter from the drizzle, the stink of urine and worse. But he needed to be ready for his sister.

First with one hand, then with the other, Easy reached up above his head, in an attempt to stretch some of the stiffness out of his bones. Slowly, aching, he folded from the waist, lurched towards his toes. His trainers and trackies were filthy and torn, his hands were dirty, covered in cuts ... from his cross-country trek. His face was probably as bad. *Would Trix recognize him?*

He was stuffed if she didn't.

Gradually, as he made his way along to the end of the derelict building, the tight joints and aching muscles began to loosen up and lose some of their painfulness. Swinging his arms a few times for good measure, he hunkered down in the shadows to wait.

As Trix walked by with her friends, he waited for the moment her gaze alighted on his face – a beggar boy holding out his hand. A wink did the trick. She looked fit to freak, but masked the shock well from her friends.

'Easy!' Moments later, she came charging back up the street.

Putting a finger to his lips, Easy stepped back into the shadows. There was a gap in the corrugated tin, a small space on the other side cluttered with rubbish and rubble.

Trix followed him in. 'Easy!' she panted again. She stood motionless, staring at him. 'What ... what's happened to you? You look ... *terrible*. Are you all right?'

Easy nodded. 'A little cold, a little soggy ... and very, very *tired*.' His sister looked more gaunt than he remembered. She seemed wary of him. He grinned and held out his arms. 'But apart from that ...'

'Eaurgh!' Trix pulled a face. 'Sorry, but –' she grinned – 'not in your present state. I'll give the hug a miss if you don't mind.' Taking hold of his hands, she squeezed them. 'God, Ease, these last few weeks have been terrible. What on earth have *you* been up to?'

'I ran away.' Easy glanced at his filthy clothes. 'They'll be looking for me, that's why I haven't been home. I had to escape ... from Gunman Reds. Can you believe it! *Me*, of all people.'

"The apartment's being watched,' said Trix, 'twenty-four hours a day.' As he had feared. 'Dad's been arrested,' said Trix.

'What! How come?'

Trix's face darkened. 'He was charged with theft, fraud and *conspiracy*. Dad! Can you imagine?' She sighed and shook her head. 'Then, yesterday, police and club officials arrived, looking for you.' Trix's eyes narrowed, gauging his reaction.

'What did they say?'

'That you weren't well. That you suffered some kind of breakdown. They spoke to Mum in private, but I listened at the door. They said you were dangerous and unstable. Something about you going berserk and attacking trainees and a member of staff?'

'What!' Easy laughed. 'What a load of rubbish! They've made it all up. Just like they've made up that rot about Dad.'

'I thought they must have.' Trix smiled. 'But I'm glad to hear you say so, all the same. What's going on, Easy?'

'I need your help.'

'*Ahhh-shoo!*' Curled up, foetal, in the shadowy place he'd arranged to meet his sister, Easy blew his nose, shivered, then sneezed again. The 'flu. That was all he needed. '*Ahhh-choo!*' It had to be – he had all the symptoms: aching bones and muscles, shivering fits, sneezing, hot and cold, headaches. In the last twenty-four hours, it'd really taken hold. Hardly surprising, given that he'd physically exhausted himself, eaten nothing for more than two days, then lain around in light, damp clothes in the cold drizzle.

He was down to the last of his tissues. Trix's sweetie money could have been better spent, but the prospect of blowing his nose on damp clothes or newspaper had really been too grim.

'*Ahh-aaaah-aaah-ah-choo!*' Every time he sneezed, it seemed to shake up the aches in his bones and muscles and make them hurt more. '*Ahhh-choo!*' The last tissue was gone.

'Easy ...' Trix scuttled into the shadows. 'Ah ... there you are.' She held out a bag. 'Clothes, food, tissues and plasters. Oh yeah ...' She dug her hands in a pocket. '... and here ...' She held out some coins. 'It's all I had. Without involving Deena or Mum, I couldn't get hold of any more.'

'You've done brilliantly. *Ahhh-choo!*'

'Bless you!'

'Thanks ...' Easy rummaged in the bag for fresh tissues. He blew his nose and ripped open a bag of cookies. Two biscuits in his mouth, he offered the bag to Trix.

'No thanks. I ate breakfast.' Sweeping dirt and rubbish off an old tyre, Trix sat. 'Sorry I'm late – I had to come by an odd route. I thought I was being followed.' Trix peered at her brother. 'Easy, sorry – but you look even worse than before!'

'Thanks.' Easy munched. 'Just the boost I needed.'

'Yeah, well – yesterday I assumed it was all dirt. But now that you've had a bit of a clean up ....' Trix pulled a face. 'You really don't look well.'

'*Ahhh-choo!*'

'Easy, you're *ill*.'

'A bit snuffly.'

'You should see a doctor.'

'It's just a cold.'

'Don't be ridiculous …' Trix touched her brother's forehead. 'You're hot. Something's wrong with you. You're shivering. You have to see someone. You must have a fever. There are all sorts of viruses going round. It's been on the news.'

'People are looking for me.' Easy dragged off his damp shirt. 'A doctor might report me if I visit. It's just a chill, Trix. I'll get something from the chemist.' He pulled on a dry hooded top. Fleece.

'There's a towel in the bag. Dry yourself first.' Trix turned away from him. 'You may as well put on dry trackie bottoms and underpants, while you're at it. I'm not looking.'

Easy clenched his jaw to stop his teeth chattering. The fleecy top was warming him already. But Trix was right: the rest of his wet clothes now felt worse. So, while Trix filled him in on what had been happening while he'd been away, he yanked off his soggy trainers, tugged off his socks, peeled off his clothes and began drying his body with the towel.

'Easy …'

'Uh-huh.' Easy pulled on the fresh, dry underpants.

'Easy …' There was alarm in Trix's voice.

'What?' One leg in his trackie bottoms, Easy staggered to keep balance as he looked up. He peered at the figure standing silhouetted against the entrance.

His heart sank. *'Ahhh-choo!'* The sneeze nearly threw him off balance.

'Easy, I'm sorry …' Trix's voice quivered. 'I was certain no one followed me, honest. I really tried my best …'

'Hello, Easy.'

Easy wobbled on one leg. 'What are you doing here?'

Deena stepped round her younger sister. 'I might ask you the same thing. You were supposed to be training at Nuvillage.'

Tugging up the trackie bottoms, Easy fastened them at his waist. 'It didn't work out,' he said. *'Ahhh-choo!'* He blew his nose and set about putting on his socks and trainers.

'Mum has been going frantic.' Deena's face contorted. 'As if having the police and IFFA agents coming round in the middle of the night isn't bad enough. You've no idea what it's been like: banging on the door, waking us all up and asking loads of questions about Dad and what he's been doing since he quit his job at Gunman Reds.'

Deena stepped towards him, thrusting an accusing finger. 'Now you have to go and double the strife by running amok at training camp: assaulting people, breaking into their medical building and God knows what else. You absconded under contract, stole stuff and went on the run. You idiot! What's *wrong* with you?' She scowled. 'Believe me – they are *not* happy.'

A cold wind blew in off the street. In spite of the dry clothes, Easy felt its chill to his bones. He shivered.

'Next thing you know, my baby sister will be under arrest, for consorting with a criminal, harbouring a fugitive.'

'*Our* baby sister. At least I can trust her.'

Trix scowled. 'I'm not anybody's *baby*.'

'Mum'll do her nut if she finds out,' said Deena. 'Don't you think she's got enough on her plate without you trying to rope Trix in on your trouble? *Hand yourself in.*'

'That's what you want, isn't it?' Easy glared. How much simpler it'd be if he could just explain everything, but Dad had made him promise. 'You take the club's point of view very readily for someone who's never professed to be a big fan of the game, let alone Gunman Reds.'

'So?'

'How come you're so keen to have me back there? How did they track me down in the first place? How did they find out where we'd moved to, Deena? Could it have had something to do with a boy called Fez?'

Deena's face darkened. He'd touched a raw nerve. She stepped forward threateningly. 'Are you accusing me?'

Easy didn't move.

'You're the criminal and trouble-maker,' snapped Deena. 'They're more than keen to get their hands on you. There's a reward for information leading to your recovery.'

'Surely, even *you* wouldn't sink that low.'

Deena jabbed a finger. 'Don't bank on it.'

Easy bowed his head. 'OK … look, I'll sort things

out.' He forced contrition into his voice. It had to be convincing. 'I'll apologize. I'll go back to the club. Please ... don't tell anyone you've seen me. Give me a little time. I will go back, but I need to do this my own way.'

'Twenty-four hours.'

'What!'

Deena nodded. 'We're taking a risk just talking to you here and now. You're a fugitive. The next time the detectives or the agents drop by to question us, I'm not going to lie on your behalf, Easy Linker. You'd better sort out whatever it is you need to sort out in that befuddled brain of yours, and get yourself back to face the music. Think about Mum. Think about all the stress and worry this is causing her. It's bad enough, the business with Dad. You have to hand yourself in.'

'Yeah, you're right.' Easy nodded. 'OK ... I'll do it.'

'Come on, Trix.' Deena tugged at her sister's sleeve as she headed for the street. 'We're both going be late for school.'

Trix scuttled over to her brother. 'I know you didn't do anything bad,' she whispered. She hugged him, rubbing his back and arms. 'God, you're cold! Use some of the money to get something hot inside you. Good luck. Take care.' Kissing his cheek, she turned and hurried off after her sister.

Bacon, eggs, sausage, beans, tomatoes, fried bread, mushrooms and toast. When had breakfast ever tasted so good? Head down, heaping food on to his fork, Easy had cleared nearly half the plate before taking a breather. He sat back and looked around. Most of the customers were staring up at the overhead screen, transfixed by the News Channel, eating with their mouths open. Not a pretty sight.

'Police are baffled how thieves gained access to the MP's home, on this prestigious Primrose Hill development. As you can see, the entire compound is surrounded by a high brick wall, topped with razor wire and other security devices.'

Easy drained his mug of sweet tea and called for another. He let the chitter-chatter and the sound from the screen wash over him. His appetite had vanished.

Arriving with a fresh mug of tea, the waitress took away the plate which he'd pushed to one side. His stomach felt ugly. He was grateful to see the food go. He thanked her and settled back to gaze at the screen.

'One thing is clear – this was no opportunist break-in. With such a sophisticated security set up, the gang that targeted Munro Sweet's property were pretty determined.'

Easy was on the edge of his seat. *Munro Sweet* – the MP Dad had mentioned.

'Mr Sweet, any thoughts on what these burglars might have been after?'

The man with a thick head of white hair shrugged. 'Not really.' His soft, sonorous voice oozed charm and calm. 'Though if they hadn't been disturbed when they were … who knows what they might have taken.'

'They ransacked your house?'

Sweet nodded. 'Turned it upside down. They fled empty-handed apparently, but then there was little worth stealing. It's not as if I have a safe containing priceless jewels. The walls of my home are not hung with a valuable art collection. I've lived here for the last nine years. I chose this place with its very visible security not because of any need to protect property or valuables, but purely and simply because I'm an MP.'

'So, no sign so far of anything going missing. Nothing? Not a thing?'

Sweet nodded. 'As far as I can tell, not at this stage.'

'They escaped …'

'Out through this window here, along the drive to that house over there, number seventeen. There they boosted the car parked outside, turned it round and took off through the big gates without stopping.'

'And I believe they were armed?'

'That's right,' said Sweet. 'Both men were carrying hand-guns. Neither took a shot at me, thank God. But the security guard who challenged them was extremely lucky not to have been more seriously wounded. That's what makes me suspect this was more than a simple failed robbery.'

'You think this raid was politically motivated?'

Sweet shrugged and smiled. 'As an opposition MP, I've always considered it my duty to speak my mind. If they were looking for valuables, they were seriously ill-informed.'

13

SWEET

A slim sliver of new moon hung in the clear sky. The night was cold. It wasn't just him shivering, it really was cold. Every breath clouded in the chill air.

Easy brushed aside low branches, pushing his way through dense rhododendron. Sweet's neighbours' house loomed ahead, recognizable from the interview on the News Channel. And there, next to it, framed by lush vegetation, the front door he was aiming for. Now, if he could just keep from sneezing …

The whole compound was quiet as a graveyard, the close even quieter. His breathing sounded loud and laboured, the only sound in the silent night. Apart, that was, from the occasional diesel-engine whirr of passing security patrol vehicles.

What was his next move? Getting inside the high-security compound really hadn't been so difficult. Any idiot watching the news item could have worked it out. But the house – given what had just happened – that was a risk too far.

Easy was still peering out through the rhododendron leaves, weighing up the various possible approaches, when a stately-looking car purred up the close and parked outside the MP's house. Briefcase in hand, Munro Sweet emerged from the back seat. He waved goodnight to the driver and walked up the path to his front door. The car purred away.

Would there be extra security? Hidden guards and cameras? Only one way to find out. Checking one last time that all was clear, Easy sprinted across the road and dived for the bushes beside Sweet's porch. Crouching, he held his breath and listened for any sign that he'd been spotted. He peered from behind the bush. No patrol cars, no twitching curtains. OK.

A stretch. A press of the bell. Then back under cover behind the bush. He held his breath.

Footsteps sounded in the hallway. Locks clunked. The front door opened a short way ... snagging against a hidden chain. 'Hello ...?' Sweet's voice sounded puzzled rather than wary. '*Hello* ... anybody there?'

Easy quickly stepped out to where he could be seen. 'I need to talk to you.'

'How did you get in here?' Sweet peered.

'It wasn't difficult,' said Easy. 'You need better security.'

'Who are you?'

'Easy Linker.' Easy stepped closer. 'I need help. My dad mentioned your name.'

Sceptical eyes squinted through the gap. 'Round the back,' hissed Munro Sweet.

'*Ahhh-choo!*' Easy sneezed, shivered and sneezed

again. Throughout his tale, Sweet had sat in silence, the shotgun balanced across his knees. 'After what happened last night,' he'd explained, letting him in through the french windows, 'I can't be too cautious.' The shotgun, Easy realized, was a protection against *whoever*. Including him.

Easy ran his fingers over the small, coin-sized bump in his jacket lining. The micro-disc. 'When I saw the files for each of the *retired* players,' he continued, 'I really wanted to read them all. But there wasn't time, so I –'

'Hold it!' Sweet held up his hand. 'Pause there, young man … if you've obtained some kind of evidence, it might be better if you keep the details to yourself, for the time being.'

Easy frowned.

'Have you told anyone else?'

'No.'

'Good.' Sweet nodded. 'What people don't know, they can't tell. And that includes me.' He tapped the side of his nose. 'The fewer people who know about it, the less chance there is of it falling into the wrong hands. Whatever it is you've gotten hold of – papers, discs, whatever – hide it somewhere it won't get found.' Sweet massaged his neck. 'And while you're at it, dump any personal ID you might be carrying. Disguise yourself as far as possible and devise yourself a new name. Use an anagram of your real one, that way when you get back in touch, I'll know who you are … even if I don't recognize you.' He smiled. 'I have an anagrammatical brain!'

'You mean take the letters from "Easy Linker" and jumble them up? Like … Lee …' Easy mouthed and counted letters on his fingers. 'Lea … Nikey Lears … Niky Learse!'

'That's the idea,' said Sweet. 'The more plausible, the better.' He sighed. 'I'm sorry. This place is a target at the moment. They know my views and leanings, but as long as there's nothing here, they can't move against me. It's no good my offering to keep you here. My advice …' He leant forward, conspiratorially. '… if you haven't already hidden your evidence, that's your first priority.'

Easy nodded. No sanctuary, then. His stomach was churning. He felt sick.

Sweet was staring at him, examining him. 'What do you know about the UFL?'

'Not a lot.' Easy tried to concentrate. 'The Unaffiliated Football League … a bunch of amateurs who run their own divisions around the country. They're supposed to have a stray following in areas not served by the big official clubs. You can sometimes get their games on pirate channels. Lively crowds, but lousy camera-angles.'

Sweet smiled. 'There's a bit more to them than that. Over the years, your father's made a lot of strong connections with UFL clubs and their supporters. It might surprise you to hear this from me, a Member of Parliament but, although UFL and its activities are banned, I approve of what they're doing and what they stand for. By and large, they're good people – they believe in fair play.'

This was a surprise to Easy. He had always thought of the UFL as dangerous, anti-social, low-life types. Occasionally there'd be stories about them on the news – how one of their illegal matches had been raided by the police, a near-riot had broken out and violence had spread into surrounding areas – nearly always the poorest neighbourhoods. 'Have you had dealings with them?' he asked.

Sweet shook his head. 'My position and responsibilities make that almost impossible. But they've helped your father no end – pointing him in the direction of evidence that's going to help him expose this enhancers scandal.'

Sweet uncocked the gun. 'Through these people he's also become aware of other scams which IFFA and the big clubs have been running. Everybody's priority right now is to find out who's holding your father and where he's being held, then maybe we can work on getting him released. As long as he's in *their* hands, this whole network of contacts he's built up is extremely vulnerable.'

Rising from the chair, Sweet carried the gun over to the dresser and propped it against the side. He turned to Easy. 'You're looking poorlier by the minute. I'm worried about you. By the sound of things, you've been through no end. How about another hot drink?'

'If you don't mind …' Easy's head was swimming. Although he was shivering, he felt hot. '… I'd rather have something cold … a glass of water?'

Sweet eyed him suspiciously. 'OK. If that's what

you want. Come with me into the kitchen. Maybe you'd like something to eat?'

'I'm fine.' Easy shook his head. He felt sick. Sweet pressed a cool hand against his forehead. Refreshing.

'You're running a fever,' said Sweet. 'We need to get someone to take a look at you. The 'flu is dangerous enough. But if they were putting enhancers and God knows what else into your food ...' He shook his head gravely.

Easy pressed his cheek against the cool glass. Outside the window, amber-lit streets rolled by. Unfamiliar. Downtown. Heading for Southside.

The driver glanced in his mirror. 'You all right, son?'

Easy nodded. He wasn't. Not at all. His bones ached. His skin felt two sizes too tight. His scalp itched. He was struggling to keep everything – brain, body, and what was the other one? – together. No way was he all right. He could feel panic lurking. He had kept it at bay till now. 'It is a bit stuffy back here,' he grunted.

'I can open the window for you,' said the driver. 'Yeah?'

Easy nodded.

'But I warn you ...' The driver watched him in the mirror. '... it's pretty cold out.'

'Thanks,' said Easy. 'Just a crack. I'm feeling queasy.' His hands were sweating. The awful fluttery feeling kept returning. He could *smell* his own fear.

'Not far, now,' said the driver.

110

Easy breathed the cold damp air and lay back in the seat. It felt good. Munro Sweet had seemed an honest man. Someone you could trust. He had spoken sense: it wouldn't have done either of them any good if the authorities had come round and discovered him. Easy Linker, a Gunman renegade on the run, hiding in an outspoken opposition MP's house. Sweet had been right – it was best he go into hiding.

'Somewhere round here suit you, son?' The eyes glanced in the mirror. The cab had slowed. 'The guv'nor said to put you down outside the church.'

Easy wiped the misty glass and peered. The street appeared dark, hemmed in by high buildings. But a little further up, an enormous neon cross blazed in front of a floodlit building.

Easy nodded.

'Anywhere in particular?'

'Here'll do fine,' said Easy. The building looked like a Greek temple, steps ascended to a row of pillars at the front. Above the pillars, the triangular pediment was an enormous neon sign that filled with words and then emptied again. It wasn't like any church he'd ever seen.

14
CHURCH

Shivering in the drizzle, Easy clutched himself for warmth and climbed the steps. His body felt so tired, he could no longer tell if he ached or not. Lifting his feet to climb each step seemed a Herculean effort.

Half way up, he stopped to gaze up at the neon sign. Raising his head made him dizzy. Word by word, the sign spelled out the name of the church in stylish golden letters: Sacred … Oracular … Church … of Christ's … Eternal … Revelation.

What?! Easy blinked. The neon buzzed; he felt woozy. The first letter of each word strobed, the other letters dimmed. The initials spelled out: S–O–C–C–E–R.

SOCCER! 'What kind of place is this?'

Enter the church, take a seat in the congregation and wait for someone to approach – those had been Sweet's instructions. A password, *Game On*, would be delivered with a wink. *Let's Do It*, was the reply he had to remember.

From behind the enormous wooden doors came the muffled sound of congregational singing. Easy put his ear to the crack and listened. He'd never been to church, he didn't know what to expect. But SOCCER – what kind of a church was *that*?

The big black iron handle turned. Easy pushed. The massive door shifted and spirited voices welled out into the night.

'Walk on, walk on, with hope in your heart, and you'll never walk alone ...'

Putting all his weight against the door, Easy heaved. Reluctantly, the door gave.

'... you'll ne-e-e-ver walk alone ...'

The words made his heart flutter. As they always did at Highbury when the massed ranks of supporters, home and away fans, chanted as one united voice. And here were people, on their feet, dancing around, waving their arms and singing the self-same football songs in church! That couldn't be so bad. Supporting his weary body against a pillar, Easy added his voice.

The words came to an end, the music faded out; with a cacophony of shuffling, whispering and coughing, the congregation settled back into their seats. Spotting a small space on the end of a pew, Easy scuttled and perched.

A large, black man, dressed in dark robes, climbed the stairs to the pulpit and spread his arms wide for quiet. He raised his hands towards the high vaulted ceiling and *whistled*! Two shrill, short blasts. The church filled with silence. 'Brothers and sisters ...' he boomed.

The congregation murmured their reply.

'Welcome, one and all, to our little congregation ... Allow me to introduce myself to those newcomers among you ... I am Reverend Shankly Obeah, your brother, your friend and God's Minister here in the ... Sacred Oracular Church of Christ's Eternal Revelation ...'

Easy glanced along the row, he cast his eye over the pews in front of him. This congregation wasn't tiny – it was *huge*. There had to be getting on for a thousand people. A real mixture – boys and girls, men and women right across the age range, a variety of races.

Easy rubbed his eyes. He had been cold outside, now he was feeling too warm again. His eyes were so tired, it was hard to focus. Leaning back against the pew, he peered discreetly. Most of the congregation wore evidence of their allegiance to one football club or another – replica shirts, supporters hats, scarves or t-shirts. Mostly from clubs in the BPL and the Corporates League. But there were colours he didn't recognize. He was in Southside now. UFL territory.

The Minister had already worked himself into a sweat and was building to a frenzy – haranguing his congregation about the sinfulness that had come to be associated with 'God's Game'. There was fire in the man's voice: sometimes it rolled easily, sometimes it boomed around the large space like a cannon shot. 'We must cast out the wretched twin demons – *drink* and *gambling*. It is my ministry, brothers and sisters ... my ministry and *our* duty to restore to God's Game the purity and nobility with which it was once truly blessed ...'

'*Hallelujah!*'

'Disciples of the game are disciples of the Almighty.'

'*Hal-le-loooooo-ja!*'

The music and rhythm of the Reverend Minister's voice were hypnotic. Easy found his mind wandering. He felt drowsy. The heat from the sea of bodies was stifling. Which one of these people had received a message from Mr Munro Sweet, MP? Who was going to approach him and reveal their purpose through the password? Someone already here, waiting in the congregation? Perhaps they hadn't arrived yet.

Behind the altar, one enormous stained-glass window reached up towards the rafters. It glowed brightly, illuminated by the floodlights outside the building. A black man.

Easy stared. The figure was dressed in Brazil's 1970 national soccer team colours; he was volleying a high ball. Instantly recognizable. The congregation gave a hearty '*Amen!*' The Reverend Minister rumbled on.

Easy silently mouthed the hallowed name: Edson Arantes do Nascimento, known the world over as simply *Pele*.

Stained-glass windows lit the side aisles of the church too. Closest to where he was sitting, Easy recognized famous historical figures from the British game: Sir Stanley Matthews, Sir Matt Busby, Sir Bobby Charlton and Sir Alex Ferguson. From time to time, the Very Reverend Minister pointed to the figures in these windows to illustrate some point in his sermon, referring to them as 'The Patriarchs'.

Over on the other side of the church, a pantheon of players The Minister referred to as 'latter-day saints and martyrs': Georgie Best, Tony Adams, Steve Brooks, Damon Huckerby, Brad Kowalski ... genius players whose lives had been blighted by the game. Easy knew their stories – Dad had told and retold them since before he could remember ...

The roar of the crowd echoed down the tunnel, like the baying of some awesome, terrifying monster. The sound became a chant: *'Easy! Easy! Easy!'*

Three figures stood in front of him, silhouetted against the glare of floodlights. The middle of the three turned. Easy stared. He recognized the man. He was so familiar – but not in that referee's strip. The Reverend Shankly Obeah smiled, close up and in slow-motion: two rows of shining white teeth. 'Ready?'

Easy turned to look behind. Turning his head seemed to take for ever. Two rows of players in contrasting team strips. Some shook their arms and legs, others stretched, to keep muscles warm. Some of the faces were hauntingly familiar.

Beside him, at the head of the second column, stood Jordan. Jordan grinned a big, slow, cheesy grin, turned to the referee and nodded. Easy recognized his own voice speaking. It came out slow and deep. 'Let's ... do ... it ...' It was his voice, but it wasn't. Someone was gently shaking his shoulder, shaking ... *'Game on ...'* whispered the voice. 'GAME ON ...'

*

Easy woke with a start. *The password!* A hand was on his shoulder.

'You dozed off during my sermon,' said Shankly Obeah.

Easy blinked.

'I instructed the ushers to let you sleep.' The church was dark and empty. Shankly Obeah leant forward and peered. 'And by the looks of you, I'd say a good deal more rest might be needed.' He smiled. 'Hang on in there! Shouldn't take too much longer to arrange.' The wink. 'Game on.'

'Game on?' Easy stuttered. 'Let's do it.'

Shankly Obeah nodded. 'Amen.'

15
ANAGRAM

Resiny Lake? It had a strong feel to it, but didn't really sound like a name. Sireny Lake for a girl, maybe. Sir Lee Yank ... that was striking, but unfortunately not a lot of use for a thirteen-year-old on the run. Pity.

Nyk Leasier ...Yas Lineker ... Asel Nykier ... Kyle Nasier ... Finding a plausible-sounding anagram of his name didn't seem to be much of a problem. But he was feeling woozy, the key thing was choosing one he would remember. He had nothing to write on. At least the mental effort was a distraction. It helped keep him awake and on his feet.

Rain began to bucket down. Pulling his collar up tight around his neck, Easy dashed for shelter. How come he always seemed to end up back outside in the cold and wet? He was shivering, but his throat felt unbelievably dry. He gazed thirstily at puddles, tried to catch raindrops with his tongue. Like some reptile, like some ...

Snake!

Easy began frantically trying to rearrange the

letters of his name. S – n – a – k – e. *Yes!* Why hadn't he thought of that? What did it leave? L – i – r ... *no, that didn't go anywhere.* R – i – l ... e – y. *Perfect!* That was it. All ten letters. Snake Riley! Cool ... believable ... *memorable.* His new name.

The rain had grown more ferocious. Pressed against the wall, Easy watched the downpour, toying with his new name. Across the street, a boisterous group of boys and girls ran, laughing, cursing and screaming, through the rain. They halted in front of a small neon sign that said simply: 'Subterrania'. Below it were the words 'Yoof Bar – No Drugs. No Alcohol' and a flashing arrow pointing to a basement staircase. The group descended. Music, voices and laughter spilled out into the night.

Easy peered through the rain at the other dark doorways lining the street. On more than one occasion since his escape from Nuvillage, he'd had the sense that someone was following him. But there were no shadowy figures sheltering along the street. Just jumpiness. The sooner he got shelter, the better.

Midnight, in the alleyway behind the church. The appointed time and place. Reverend Shankly Obeah was arranging for someone to meet him. Hopefully, they'd have somewhere he could stay out of the rain at least long enough to get some strength back. *Then, what was he going to do?*

Braving the rain, Easy made a dash for the 'Subterrania' sign. He hurried down the steps; warmth, lively music and laughter rushed at him as the doors swished open. He stepped inside. The lighting was soft, subdued – no ceiling fixtures, just the glow from wall-mounted gaming machines and floodlit table-football tables. The drinks bar gently hummed and luminesced.

Easy felt eyes watching him; as he looked around, they flitted away. He was the *outsider*. Too young, maybe, too fresh-faced? They were probably all regulars. Ignoring the glances, he made his way to the bar.

Bloodshot eyes, ringed round with deep dark circles, glared at him from behind the counter. A gaunt face, messy, matted hair. Desperate stare. Easy glowered back, prepared for confrontation. But the youth didn't bat an eyelid. Didn't move, didn't speak, didn't twitch.

'*Ai-choo!*'

Easy clutched the bar. The youth behind the bar had sneezed too. *His reflection!* He looked dreadful: wan and haggard. Like one of those kids that slept in shop doorways and lived on the streets – too old for his years. Way too old. The jumpy feeling, that awful shaky something-really-bad's-about-to-happen feeling was creeping back up on him.

'Drink?' The barman eyed him suspiciously.

Easy's mouth made a dry *clacking* sound. 'Glass of water,' he croaked.

The barman placed the glass on the bar and stood back, arms folded, watching.

Now the water was there in front of him, Easy's thirst had vanished. He forced himself to sip. He did feel hot, but ... Suddenly, he knew he was going to be sick. The room started to heave, it tilted like a ship. Pushing away, he lurched for the toilets.

Ouch! Easy opened his eyes. Moving his head *hurt*. He had thrown up first, he remembered that much. His stomach muscles ached from the empty retching. Now he'd come round, surprise surprise, he was cold again. Shivering. He checked his watch. Couldn't have been unconscious for very long. Perhaps the worst was over, perhaps at last the sickness was passing?

The effort it took to climb to his feet promised otherwise. Muscle ache. Shaking. Teeth chattering. Whatever it was was still in him. The toilet bowl brought back waves of queasiness. He pressed the flush, pushed down the seat and slumped, exhausted. A slow tear trickled down his cheek. Then another. He could taste the salt in his mouth. It had come to this.

This struggle wasn't just about him.

Closing his eyes he pictured Jordan: on the toilet, magazine in his lap, shorts round his ankles, grinning. Ajax Morayne: writhing and screaming, strapped to the recliner. Dad: perched at his bedside, grave, sorrowful.

Easy braced himself against the wall and pulled himself upright. *So weak.* A heave, up on to the toilet seat. A fumble in the lining of his jacket for the microdisc. Reaching up, he placed it on top of the cistern. There. Something done at last.

Washing his face in the sink, he straightened up and walked back out into the bar.

'You're new round here.'

Easy nodded. Though he turned his head slowly, the room still rocked. She was tall for a girl. Older than him. Big smile. Pierced lip. Keloid scarring on the cheeks.

'I'm here night and day,' said the girl. 'I know everybody.' She looked him up and down. 'You meeting somebody? Hope you don't mind me saying this but, well – you don't look all that.'

'No ...' grunted Easy. 'I know. I look rough. Came in to get out rain.' He laughed weakly. 'I don't think I'm very well.'

'I know just the thing.' The girl touched his arm. 'A drink that kills it stone dead.' Whistling shrilly, she ordered a 'Zombie Special'. 'It's got everything!' she said. 'It's not just a pick-you-up, it's a rip-you-right-out-of-your-boots-and-shake-the-living-daylights-back-into-you.'

'What's in it?' said Easy.

'Nothing illegal.' The girl grinned. 'Ginseng. Plenty of fresh caffeine, and enough herbs and spices to blow your socks off.'

The youth behind the bar brought her a coffee.

The girl winked at Easy. 'Yours'll take a little longer to prepare. Come and tell me what you think.' She nodded towards the rear of the crowded basement. 'I've got to get back, I'm afraid. I'm on duty in the parlour tonight.'

'Parlour?' grunted Easy.

'Tattoos,' said the girl. 'What's your name?'

'Ea –,' Easy stopped himself. 'Snake ... Snake Riley.'

'Snake ...' The girl tried the sound of the word. She smiled and turned. 'You know where I am.'

What was one more pain? Clutching his arm, Easy staggered through the rainy night. Drenched clothes clinging to his body like a lead wet-suit, he bumped against walls, side-swiped lamp-posts, collided with old boxes and rubbish strewn along the kerb.

He must have looked like a drunk. The contents of his head were sloshing around. He was bracing himself for the spin. The one thing he knew was that he must be in that alley by midnight. He had to be there. Everything depended on it. Nothing else mattered.

He stopped, clinging against a corner, and gasped great lungfuls of air. But the watery world kept swimming. He peered through the murk. *Where was this? Where was the church ... the blazing cross? Was this the right direction?*

What was *that*?! Easy twisted round. Footsteps? Someone moving in the shadows behind? The street spun and wobbled. He was seeing double. Triple. The pain in his arm exploded. His yelling echoed down the street.

Bingo. The church. Not far now, just keep going. Keep on *going.* Staggering off the kerb, he splashed into a puddle and on across the road. Someone was following him, no doubt about it.

Nothing lit the street up the side of the church. As

he trudged towards the entrance to the alley, the street-lamp glow grew dim. His heartbeat swelled in the darkness. Louder and louder. Panic exploded. That sound again! Unmistakable – *someone was following*. They were close, *very* close.

Run!

Fear gripped his chest, his arms wouldn't swing, his lungs rasped. If something happened now, there'd be no witnesses. No one would know. He forced his legs to pump, forced his arms to swing, forced lungs to breathe. Footsteps splashed and pounded on the street behind him. They were gaining on him. Coming *closer* …

Easy turned into the side-alley. Staggering, hobbling, limping, gasping. His panicking heart was trying to rip its way out of his chest. Glancing back, he crashed into something solid, tripped and tumbled into the hard wet. Someone screamed.

As he glanced up, a shape moved against the darkness. He tried to struggle to his feet, but arms and legs were shaking too badly. His heart was deafening. Behind him, the footsteps came closer. Even louder, a horrible, rasping sound …

Death.

16

SNAKE

The end of a sleep. A long, long sleep. Even time had been sleeping. That's what it had felt like.

Endless blankness. Like a long, bare, concrete tunnel, soft fluorescent lighting. No memories – though he knew he'd been alive once, he knew something had happened. Occasionally, hints and whispers of a past intruded into the blankness, but nothing stayed.

It was quieter than hush in that place. Cut off from everything. Just gently cruising through. No beginning. No end. No sound.

Totally still. At peace. But always a sense of moving forward.

Then ...

... long after it had lasted for ever ...

BANG.

A door closing. He opened his eyes.

A bare room: windows, chair, picture, bedside table, lamp, bed. Two ridge-like formations stretched out beneath the covers. *Legs*. The room wasn't empty after all. He tilted his head.

Above the legs, on top of the covers, two arms, crossed at the wrist. The one on the left was connected by tubes and wires to something behind him, out of sight. The right one was tattooed: a gently spiralling pattern, round and round, it thickened towards the top. He dropped his head.

At the shoulder, the coil extended out across the chest, in an elaborate representation of a snake's head. *A rattler?*

Like some rusty old machine, squeaking and creaking back into life after years of disuse, his mind began to flex. If this was the only body in the room and he was looking down on it … *then it must be his own!* The snake tattoo was on *his* arm.

He stared down at the end of the bed, the small peak where the covers were raised up. A foot. He willed it to *wiggle*. The peak moved. Toes. *His* toes. He turned his attention to the arms. Raising the tattooed one, he moved the hand up towards his face. The arm felt stiff, it moved clumsily. He closed his eyes, letting the fingers probe. Mouth, nose, eyes … ears … nothing where he'd expected eyebrows. The scalp was covered with just the faintest bristles of hair. Who was he?

'Aha!'

His eyes opened.

'Snake!' A bespectacled man stood beaming at the foot of the bed. 'How are you feeling?'

Snake. That was his name – Snake? 'I …' His vocal cords rasped. His voice croaked. 'I'm not sure.'

The man dragged the chair over to the bed and sat. 'You've been through a bit of a rough time.' The words were warm, the voice melodious. 'You'll be feeling very weak. What can you remember?'

He tried to push his mind back. But there was only the long blankness. 'Nothing. Where am I?'

'This is a hospital. The Bethlehem. I'm Dr Petit. Our unit specializes in young homeless and drug-addicted victims. You were brought to us, flitting in and out of consciousness.'

Young ... homeless ... drug-addicted ... Was *that* what he was? 'You called me *Snake* ...' There was a familiarity about the word.

Petit shrugged. 'You weren't carrying any ID. We were rather hoping you might be able to tell us who you were.'

He felt a pain in his bones. He clutched himself.

Petit leant forward, took his hand. 'Don't worry. You're going to feel the odd aches and pains for a few days yet. But the worst is over.' He nodded to the tubes and wires. 'We've had you on a drip for ten days now. This is your first real lucidity. It'll come and go to begin with.'

'I don't understand.'

'You're being treated for withdrawal – a number of very toxic performance-enhancers, plus various acclimatizers, reaction-suppressants, pacifiers and brain-washing drugs.' Petit removed his glasses, rubbed his brow and replaced them. 'There are no signs of permanent damage. Memories should return – it just takes time.' He smiled again. The dark brown eyes glanced at the tattoo. 'The staff nicknamed you *Snake* because of that. Until now, *Snake* has been the only recognizable sound you've uttered.

'Snake Riley ...'

Pain in his bones. Pain in spasming muscles. His gut twisted. His head burst. He was running through rainy darkness. What was he running from? Where was he running to?

Running in pain, gasping, running, running ... and then *nothing*.

Trace back. Rewind the film. Staggering along the dark wet streets, his head spinning, body aching. What came before?

A noisy place, crowded with young people, a few perhaps his own age but mostly older. Music. A bar. Kids playing table-football, laughing and joking. And in a small room at the back – a girl. The tattooist! That was *him*, out of his face, head and eyebrows shaved – part of the disguise – lying on the recliner, looking down from the ceiling mirror. The girl leaning over him, tattooing his arm with a snake. Snake.

Floodgates opened. Names, sounds and images came pouring in. Ajax Morayne, the Gunman star, screaming in agony, strapped to a recliner. A freckle-faced boy grinning, sitting on a toilet with his shorts round his ankles – *Jordan*. The strange church with the weird stained-glass windows. The wild preacher sermonizing about football – *was that real or a dream*? Munro Sweet, MP. Trix and Deena – his sisters. Nuvillage. Mum ... Dad.

The memories slotted themselves into place. He was a fugitive. He had tried to disguise himself, changed his name. Now he was Snake. Snake Riley.

Dr Petit examined the clipboard, then replaced it on its hook at the end of the bed. 'How's our patient feeling today?' He made his way over to the machines which the wires and tubes were connected to. Peering over his spectacles, he examined the displays.

'Better.' Snake pushed himself up in the bed. *Exhausting*. 'Sleep helped. Maybe the aches and spasms aren't quite so bad.'

'Good.' Seating himself on the edge of the bed, Petit cracked one of his broad smiles. 'That's what we'd hoped. Don't expect to be returned to full strength overnight, but all the signs are excellent. You're on the mend. How about the memories?'

'Yep.' Snake nodded. 'They're returning. I remember some stuff.'

Petit folded his arms. 'Here at the Bethlehem, we have a strict policy of confidentiality. But you should be careful what you tell people.' The warm smile. 'Even me, I'm afraid.'

Snake shifted his weight, trying to get comfortable.

'You've been through a lot,' said Petit. 'Your body's been through some of the worst ... you're only young. You've got to protect yourself. The way we do things here – we try to help people. Not just fix them up and chuck 'em back out on the streets. Take your time. If you want to talk ...' He nodded. 'When you think you're ready ... *only* when you think you're ready.'

'Thanks. I feel like I've been away a long time.'
Snake sighed. 'D'you like football?'

Petit laughed. 'Do I *like* it!' His eyes sparkled. 'How
can anyone *like* football? You either love it or ...' He
waved a dismissive hand. '... you're one of those
other *peculiar* people.'

Snake laughed.

'They just don't get it.' Petit shook his head. 'And
are their lives poorer, sadder, thinner, *meaner* ...? I
think so! What team do you support?'

'Gunman Reds.' Snake held his gaze. 'Last thing I
remember, they had the number-one slot. How are
they doing?'

Petit grinned. 'Still there. Do you play?'

Snake nodded.

'What position?'

Snake shrugged.

'Don't remember?' said Petit.

'No,' said Snake. 'It's not that.' He smoothed the
covers. 'I'm adaptable.' Time to reinvent himself. 'I
had this coach one time ... actually – my dad. He
showed me there was this way you could play.'

Petit nodded.

'It's a style I developed. *We* developed. With the
right team, I like to play floating playmaker – a kind
of trouble-shooter. Weaving my way through the
opposition.' Snake squiggled his finger over the cover.
'Always with a sting in my tail.' He glanced up.

Petit's face was alight. He glanced at the tattoo.
'Hence the name?'

Snake nodded.

'This I have to see!' Petit got to his feet. 'Such certainty!' He stretched. 'You've whet my appetite, young man. I'm practically licking my lips. I know when someone knows their game.' He winked. 'We'll have to get you into rehab. The physio team can start on you tomorrow, *early*.'

Snake felt sleepy muscles stir. His stretch became a yawn.

'But first – a good night's sleep.' Petit stifled his own yawn. 'Yeah?'

Snake nodded. His eyes were feeling heavy.

At the door, Petit turned, hand hovering over the light-switch. 'I think I might have just the team for you.'

Snake sat up. 'Who's that?'

'Not tonight.' Petit smiled. 'Tomorrow, I'll tell you about them.' He turned out the light. 'They call themselves the Warriors.'

17

WALWORTH WARRIORS

Two days after he returned to the world, the long process of recovery began for real. At the end of the first week, the physios and nurses were astonished by his progress: he'd attacked the training exercises with such zeal and energy, he surprised even himself.

It hadn't been easy. Every evening at the end of the daily exercise classes, the massage and manipulation, he had gone to bed aching and exhausted. But the pains had been different from those brought on by the withdrawal. The enhancers had come close to doing him in. The knowledge that his body was getting clean, detoxifying, regrowing its strength drug-free, now helped him keep going. That and the doctor's encouragement and enthusiasm.

After early progress, football training had quickly been introduced into his routine. Little by little, in the yard at the back of the ward, he had revived old skills and increased his speed and stamina. Nearly three weeks into recovery, Petit had announced it was time – they were going to visit the club.

Home territory for Walworth Warriors FC was a run-down part of Southside, about a mile from the river. According to Petit, it had once been an area of corpulent offices and high-rise housing, but the offices had long since closed down. The apartment towers had seen better days too. The Warriors' HQ and training camp were based in a disused shopping centre. The Castle.

Snake and the doctor were riding there by tram.

It was Snake's first day out of the hospital. The world looked crisp and fresh. But it was cold. He stared through the window at the passing streets. Crowds bustled at the mouth of a busy street market.

'East Street,' said Petit. 'The heartland of the Warriors' support. The streets and estates of this neighbourhood are their main recruiting-ground.'

Snake turned. 'How's the team doing?'

Petit cracked one of his big grins. Proud. 'Like your team – top of the league.'

Snake gave him a cautionary glance. 'A lot can happen – there's still games left to play.'

'The Warriors play in the London league. UFL teams don't have the money to travel. If we want to get about the country we have to use the B-roads like Mr and Mrs Joe Public.'

B-roads were B for 'Bad'. None of them had been repaired for years. Many were unusable by all but the most robust vehicles – four-wheel drives and army surplus. For people without wealth, they were the sole means of getting about the country. Access to the fast track was available only to those with credit.

Snake frowned. 'So UFL teams from the London region never get to play those from other cities?'

'Strictly speaking – yes.' Petit leant forward. 'But UFL teams are largely made up of amateurs. Few players are lucky enough to be semi-pro, so every UFL club needs to find revenue during the closed season.'

'So?'

'So in the closed season, clubs have taken to going off on small tours, travelling to a region, then playing matches on a winner-takes-the-takings basis against all the local sides. A team on a good run can make money. Nothing huge, but enough to tide them over.' Petit peered. 'Next stop's ours.'

Drab buildings and desolate streets. Snake caught sight of his reflection: skull freshly shaved like a Buddhist monk's. It still surprised him when he glimpsed himself unexpectedly. He didn't recognize what he saw, still didn't see the smooth skull and think – *that's me*. That was good. He stroked his head. If he didn't recognize himself, maybe others wouldn't either.

'The Warriors started off as a casual side,' said Petit. 'Myself and the good Baron got a bunch of lads together. I'd been trying to organize some of my patients and he'd been working on a similar idea with local lads.'

'Who's the Baron?'

Petit tapped the end of his nose. 'You'll meet him soon enough. This'll be the team's second full season in the league. We'd been going for less than six months when we applied to join.'

'And now you're top.' Snake nudged the doctor with his elbow. ' Not bad!'

The mall and its shops had long since been stripped of their trappings and fittings. Whole frontages had been demolished, rain had worked its way down from gaping holes in the building's roof, paint had peeled, masonry had crumbled, raw concrete was everywhere exposed.

Snake followed Petit down a dead escalator. Naked light-bulbs hung from wires draped round damp-ravaged pillars or dangled from high ceilings. Ahead of them their escorts, two wild-looking, scruffily dressed boys, held open battered doors that led to a basement. Spray-painted across the wall above the doors was the greeting: 'Welcome to The Castle, Home of Walworth Warriors'. A skewed sign hung below. An elephant with a miniature castle on its back.

Petit paused in front of the doors. He turned and looked up. Above them a courtyard space rose up high to the badly holed roof, three floors above. He nodded towards the far corner balcony. 'That's the nerve-centre, up there. Baron's office. The rest of the squad are quartered around the central atrium.'

Snake glanced across at the makeshift home someone had constructed in gutted shop premises just a few metres from where he stood. 'What – the whole team lives and sleeps here?' It wasn't exactly luxurious.

Petit nodded. 'Like I told you – UFL teams are poor, unlicensed and essentially illegal. Clubs like the

Warriors have little option but to base themselves in places like this. Most of the time it suits the authorities to turn a blind eye to their activities. They just let them get on with it. But if UFL clubs try to step out of the darkness and establish themselves in more permanent, legitimate premises, the authorities clamp right down on them.'

At the bottom of several flights of bare concrete stairs, the escorts again held doors open. Snake and Petit stepped out into a wide, cavernous space. An underground car park lit by fluorescent lights. Excited voices echoed off concrete walls, floor, ceiling. A small group of boys were chasing a ball, dodging and darting in and out between a row of pillars. Others were engaged in ball-skills practice and fitness exercises. Snake turned to Petit. 'This is where the Warriors train?'

'And *play*,' said Petit. 'This is their home ground.'

'Their *pitch*?'

Petit nodded. 'Come on, time for some introductions.'

Snake followed, watching as boys practised long low passes – the ceiling meant there wasn't room to lob the ball, so height control was vital. The pitch was marked out with lines of bright paint. He stopped and stared. 'There are pillars in the middle of the pitch!' Three pairs of them. He'd played on some dodgy pitches in his time, but this had to take the biscuit.

'Ah!' Petit chuckled. 'You've spotted one of the little idiosyncrasies of our ground.'

'Little!' Snake pointed. 'Six enormous great pillars!'

'We removed as many as we could. Those ones have to stay, they provide structural support to the building.' Petit shrugged. 'UFL clubs, especially those in the London League, don't have a lot of choice when it comes to pitches. There are worse ones than this, believe me. It all adds to the colour and excitement of UFL games.' He chuckled again. 'Players have to be that bit more adaptable. You'll see. I think you're really going to fit in here.'

'Greetings!' The deep voice boomed. A large man, tall and *wide*, walked towards them, arms spread in a welcoming gesture.

Petit and the large man shook hands and embraced. Petit turned to Snake. 'This is the man.'

'John Baron.' The large man held out his hand. 'Known by all as the *Baron*. You can call me what you like, but please don't call me "Sir".'

'Snake,' said Snake, shaking the offered hand.

Baron smiled. 'Pleased to make your acquaintance, young man.' He placed a hand on Petit's shoulder. 'So what have you brought me, comrade?'

'Snake's one of my patients,' said Petit. 'He started rehab only three weeks ago, but watching him at work in the hospital yard, I'd say he's an exceptional talent.'

'Runs rings round you, does he?' Baron laughed a big rolling laugh. 'That's hardly saying much, these days.'

'Take a look,' said Petit. 'Try him out. See for yourself.'

'Warri*OOOOrs*!' The Baron waved for the players to gather round.

18

SIX-A-SIDE

The Warriors were the strangest, roughest-looking team Snake had ever set eyes on. Though all of them were dressed in dark colours, that was the only consistency to their appearance. In any team you'd expect a range of physiques, but the Warriors were extreme. Practically freaks. Their goal-keeper was enormous, the wingers were leggy giants, the backs – short, compact and lightning fast.

With his shaved head and no eyebrows, Snake knew he looked weird and he had fully expected to be stared at. But when he and the Warriors first set eyes on each other, he sensed immediately why Petit had been so confident he'd feel at home. None of them so much as batted an eyelid. They stared, sure, but it was the blank, challenging stare of battle-hardened toughness.

The Warriors weren't shocked by his appearance, but then why would they be when their own skulls were also close-cropped or shaved. A few of them sported Mohicans, spikes or dreadlocks. Their faces and bodies were adorned with piercings, tattoos and keloid scars. In his present incarnation, Snake looked just like one of them. 'You'll measure up on the pitch,' said Petit. 'You're going to fit in perfectly.'

Baron set the boys playing six-a-side. Snake started off on the bench with three others. 'The squad's less than full strength,' explained Baron. 'We normally have about twenty. Our next match got postponed, so a few of the injured lads are resting up. A couple with homes to go to went visiting their families.' From time to time he made a substitution from the bench. And again, at moments when play had stopped, he gave criticism and swapped around players' positions.

Snake had been on and off the bench a couple of times. Each time the ball came his way he did his best to play in the manner he'd described to Petit – surprising the other players with lightning-fast changes of direction and snake-like dribbling – swerving round player after player, fooling them with dummies, trick moves and devious shots.

The ceiling took a bit of getting used to, though. Playing on a full-size pitch with only six on each side, there was plenty of call for the low long-shot, but it was harder than it looked. On several occasions, Snake gave away possession when his shot clipped the ceiling and fell short. What with that and trying to avoid the pillars, he had his work cut out for him. The Warriors were fit and strong, they played an extremely fast game. In spite of his three weeks' training, he was soon out of steam. Baron brought him off to take a rest.

Nicknames flew: 'Dirk!' 'Shiva!' 'Crotch!' 'Disney!'

'Spodge!' With so many players, Snake quickly lost track. But as the game progressed, one name in particular became lodged in his head. It was hard to tell, especially with the scary nose-rings and tattoo, but he felt sure that the player called 'Fluff' was a girl. He watched for a clue. Short cropped hair. No hint of breasts. Nothing girlish about the voice. Fluff was as fast, aggressive and tenacious as the others. But there was definitely something different about the way she moved.

During his third spell in the game, Snake finally scored. It was a spectacular goal and his teammates rushed to congratulate him. But not Fluff. Fluff smiled and applauded but remained at a distance.

'A good point to end on, I think.' Baron clapped his hands. 'Well done, all. And especially to Snake. A magnificent effort from someone so recently returned to the game.' He checked his watch. 'Goodness – it's late! Would one of you please take him upstairs and find him somewhere to bivvy.' Raising an eyebrow, he turned to Snake. 'I'm assuming you'd like to join our happy family?'

'Definitely,' said Snake.

As players sloped off in twos and threes, one or two hung back. Fluff marched over to Snake. 'Want me to show you around?'

Snake nodded. 'Thanks.' They were half-way up the stairs before he plucked up the courage to broach what was on his mind. 'Can I ask you something – something personal?'

Fluff's eyes narrowed. Boys ahead and behind

were in earshot. 'You mean like – Am I a girl?'

Snake felt himself blush. He nodded.

Fluff folded her arms. 'D'you have a problem with that?'

'No,' said Snake.

'Good,' said Fluff. 'Neither does the UFL.'

Living conditions at Walworth Warriors HQ were basic. Fluff had taken Snake to one of the communal sleeping areas – the shell of what had once been a shop. The players slept on hammocks, she explained, because floors on all levels of the building were prone to flooding and damp. In metal dustbins, fires fed with scavenged wood provided their only source of heating.

After a supper cooked by the three players on the nights rota, the squad settled down on old sofas and armchairs. Swapping stories and jokes, they warmed themselves around the main fire. Snake cradled a mug of sweet tea and, tired but contented, listened to their banter. His eyelids were growing heavy when Baron appeared in the firelight. The voices around the fire grew silent.

'The Warriors are a team and a family,' said Baron. 'We trust each other. We work together. We look out for each other. We play *great football*.' A chorus of voices murmured approval. 'Ours is not an easy life. We have to live on our wits, and simply too. But – we have fun!' He glanced at Snake. 'Because of the precariousness of our existence, it is vital we remain vigilant at all times.'

Snake nodded.

'The Walworth Warriors have an unspoken tradition of taking players who are ...' Baron's eyes flickered round the circle. '... how shall I put it – *in difficult circumstances*. Many of our players have come to us in need. That's not to say they don't have to fulfil the requirements for talent and ability too.'

There were grunts of agreement around the fire. Baron made a gesture. Shiva, the tall dark team-captain, rose and moved off into the shadows. Nonce, the leggy right-winger, followed him. A third boy got to his feet and added some pieces of old timber to the fire. The fire crackled, spat and blazed with renewed vigour.

'Obviously,' continued Baron, 'like any other UFL club, we have to judge very carefully who to accept as recruits. With our policies we're probably more vulnerable than most to the threat of infiltration by the authorities. Having said that, once a player is accepted into the fold, they are part of the family and, with regard to the past – it's basically no questions asked.'

Snake felt Baron's gaze fall on him.

'If you're happy with that,' said Baron, 'then there's just the matter of our little ceremony ...' He clapped his hands. Sofas and armchairs were suddenly pushed back, clearing a space around the blazing brazier.

Snake felt his skin prickle.

'Don't be alarmed,' chuckled Baron. 'You're not going to be asked to plunge your hand into burning embers or brand yourself with a red-hot poker!'

Laughter rippled round the fire.

'The Warriors may be a fearsome-looking bunch,' continued Baron, 'some of them may actually think they're tough stuff and dangerous, but it's all show and bluster. This lot are pussycats once you get to know them.' Grabbing hold of the boy nearest to him, he ruffled his hair. 'Scary appearance and ritual helps out-psych our opponents – as well as disguising identities.'

Nonce reappeared, clutching a small bundle.

'Aha!' Baron rubbed his hands. Nonce stepped forward. 'Your Walworth Warriors strip. All black.' Nonce held out shirt and shorts.

'Thank you.' Snake took it.

Baron nodded. 'Put them on over your clothes.'

Snake did as bidden.

Shiva emerged from the shadows. He was holding a football. Baron gestured. 'Take it.'

Snake did so.

'Come over to the fire,' said Baron.

Snake stepped out into the centre of the circle.

'Right, now clutch the football to your chest.' Baron mimed with his own hands. 'Press it over your heart.'

Snake copied the big man's actions.

'Empty your mind of all fears and distractions.' Baron's voice dropped to a low whisper. 'Feel your heart beating against the ball. Feel the pulse swelling inside it … filling it …'

Snake pressed the football hard against his breast and stared into the fire. He stiffened, relaxed, focused.

'Now …' Baron's voice came to him out of the darkness. 'Take your hopes … make them into a simple wish or prayer … then release it, through your heart, into the ball.'

Snake felt himself falter, conscious suddenly of the spectacle he was part of, the eyes watching from the shadows. He willed himself. Pushing the doubt away. Dad. His father's face appeared in the flames. Dad – smiling, confident, strong – as he had looked before the troubles started. 'OK …'

'You have your hope,' said Baron. 'Your prayer?'

Snake nodded. His heartbeats punched out through the football. Tight as a drum, its skin buzzed his fingers. Another twinge of self-consciousness. He imagined each pulse carrying his prayer. 'It's pumping into the ball …'

'Good.' Baron placed a hand on his shoulder. 'When you're ready, place the ball in the flames.'

Snake stepped forward through the fierceness of the heat and thrust the ball into the heart of the fire. He stood back.

The fire crackled. From within the flames came a hissing sound. The hiss grew louder. Became a shriek …

BANG! The flames were extinguished.

'Amen,' whispered a voice in the darkness.

19
CLASH

Cascading from the ruptured ceiling, rainwater splattered down off pillars and balconies, hitting the floor with a loud *splat* that echoed round the atrium.

Snake fidgeted nervously on the sofa. Most of the boys taking time off for family visits had returned the night before. Baron still hadn't announced who would be playing in the afternoon's big match. Just the *possibility* of being included in the team was making Snake twitchy.

Walworth Warriors versus Tooting Tigers. According to Fluff, previous encounters between the two arch-rivals had been the biggest earners of the season. A local derby always brought in the crowds.

Baron whistled sharply. 'Gather round … gather round.' Boys came scurrying.

Snake shuffled up against the sofa arm so Fluff could squeeze in beside him.

'First things first.' Baron peered down into the atrium. 'By the look of things, there may be problems with flooding on the pitch. So whatever you're down

145

on the rota for, it's all hands on deck before the match. I've been down to take a look – it's not too bad at the moment. We need to check all the drains and pumps are working. This is one match we can't afford to have abandoned.' Baron strode over to his armchair. 'Any questions before I announce the team?'

A boy rose to his feet. He glanced at Snake.

Snake felt the hairs bristling on the back of his neck.

'I understand we've got a new teammate.'

'That's right,' said Baron. 'Of course – some of you've been absent. You won't have been introduced.' He gestured to Snake. 'This is Snake, our latest recruit.'

'Tomtom.' The boy on his feet nodded without a hint of welcome. 'Let's hope you're not a burden.'

One by one, the other absentees stood and introduced themselves. Snake nodded to each in turn. Right through the team announcement, his eyes kept returning to the light-skinned boy. Tomtom glared back, unfazed.

'Fluff,' said Baron, 'you'll be playing right midfield.'

'Thank you,' said Fluff, winking triumphantly at Snake.

'Nonce,' continued Baron, 'you'll be playing on the right wing. Shiva, on the left.'

In spite of Tomtom's open hostility, Snake had kept his face turned towards him.

'Tomtom ...' said Baron, 'you'll be starting as striker. I want you to work closely with our new boy. Snake, I want you to adopt the roaming midfield role we tried in practice. You need to get used to each other, so let's get down to the pitch and warm up.'

Intercepting the pass, Snake switched directions and headed back towards the opposition half. The home supporters roared with delight. Spurred on by the din, he accelerated, swerving his way round one opposition player after another. But the red-shirts of Tooting were closing him down. Up ahead, two of the Warriors signalled for a pass. He dummied right, passed left. The ball sailed to Tomtom.

Tomtom swivelled and volleyed. The ball whistled past the keeper.

'*Yeeeeess!*'

Snake jogged back towards his own half. The first goal. Instead of Gunman Reds it was Walworth Warriors. But it still felt electric.

The referee's whistle blew for half-time. UFL games were played the old way with only the one break – in the middle. Applauded by the lively crowd, the two teams trotted off to the exits at either side of the pitch. Time for the coach's words of wisdom. Huddling into the stair-well with his teammates, Snake found himself a space and squatted.

Baron grinned. 'Capacity crowd!' He rubbed his hands greedily. 'You know that puts me in a good mood. Now, you've not done a bad job – you've kept the Tigers at bay magnificently, but those people out there have come to see you *win*. So that's what you have to do.'

*

The crowd had swelled since half-time. In the area around the stairs they were virtually spilling on to the pitch, there were so many still trying to get in.

Snake ran to overtake Fluff as they made their way back for the kick. 'How come people are still arriving? We must be three-quarters of the way through the match.'

'Never too late for a last-minute punt, I suppose.'

'They're gamblers?'

Fluff shrugged. 'Well, they're hardly here to watch the football!'

'I suppose not,' said Snake. 'Who would you put your money on right now?'

'I wouldn't,' said Fluff. 'Gambling stinks. Ask me who's going to win.'

'Who, then?'

'We are, stupid.' She jabbed him in the ribs. 'Pull your finger out. It's about time you *scored*, instead of just setting them up for Tomtom and Shiva.'

'What makes you think I'm capable?'

'All of us are. Besides, you're obviously not playing to your full ability.'

'What!' Snake stopped in his tracks, arms akimbo. 'What a cheek!'

'I see things others don't.'

'Really.' Snake's chuckle belied his insecurity. 'How about you score first?'

Fluff glowered. 'You know it's an automatic lifetime ban if the UFL catches you working for a syndicate?'

'What!' Snake glared back. 'You think I'm a ringer?

You think I would try to fix the result?' Fluff shrugged, turned and walked away.

The Tigers took their kick. In the confined space, the frenzied roar of the onlookers was ear-splitting. Latecomers may have come for a flutter, but the majority of the crowd were wearing colours and were noisy supporters.

3–2 down, the Tigers pushed boldly forward, looking to equalise. Short passes, kick and run, kick and run. Under Shiva's command, the Walworth forwards harried, retreated, then harried again. The midfield held their ground. The red-shirts were through the forwards and pushing on. Now Fluff went in to tackle. Tooting's tall striker had sliced round Tomtom and outrun a couple of the others. But as he tried to zip past Fluff, she got her foot to the ball and, lightning fast, poked it clean away.

As the red-shirt gasped and fell, Snake reached the ball. The Tooting hands were up for a free kick, but the ref signalled *Play on*. Snake swivelled and set off towards the opposition goal. Red-shirts fell back. Speed was the thing. Snake skirted one, then deftly another. He checked for support, but no one was up with him.

'Go it alone, Snake!' yelled Baron from the sidelines.

'*Ssssnake*,' echoed the supporters. '*Snake, Snake, Snake!*'

Gathering momentum, Snake pushed on into the opposition's half. If he could just keep it going ... He dodged left, skipped an outstretched foot. Headed round the outside of the pillar, down the wing. Red-shirts were lining up between him and the box. He took them at a run, one after another, weaving and swerving, this way then that.

The supporters' chant grew louder. Snake cut in towards the goal. From the corner of his eye he could see back-up down the wing, but there wasn't time to wait.

'Go on!' yelled Fluff. 'Take it all the way.'

Without slowing, he dummied to the right, then swung in a shot …

'*Yeeeeeesss!*'

The crowd erupted, jumping and yelling and punching the air. Pushing past stewards they invaded the pitch. Frantically the referee blew his whistle. Snake watched amazed as Baron and the Tigers' manager ran on to the pitch too, shouting and waving their arms. Something was wrong. The crowd were no longer cheering, they were running in *panic*.

Snake pushed his way over to where teammates had gathered around Baron and Petit. The din of shouting made it hard even to hear Baron's loud voice. Spotting Fluff, Snake cupped his hands round his mouth. '*What's going on?*' he yelled.

'Don't go getting excited!' Fluff grinned. 'They're not rioting over your goal – a cracker though it was. This is a *police raid!*'

20

AFTERMATH

The Baron's empty armchair was a chilling reminder.

Snake felt Fluff snuggle up. He was still shivering occasionally and, if he was honest with himself, grateful for her closeness and warmth. Warriors sat huddled together, staring numbly into the fire. Occasionally somebody would chime up with another moment recollected. In this way, a picture of events was gradually unfolding. The taller boys had seen the most.

'They were just slashing at anyone,' said Nonce. 'Kids, women, old people – they didn't care.'

The raid had been the stuff of nightmares. *Terrifying*. Pouring out into the underground arena, police in full-face helmets and riot gear had cordoned off the exits. Snake had only ever seen policemen dressed like that, behaving like that, on the screen – in movies and the news. But this had been *real*.

Using their long batons, they had herded the crowd into the centre of the pitch. Supporters who resisted or tried to fight back had been brutally bludgeoned and dragged away like corpses through police lines.

Baron had pushed through the crowd, bellowing *'Stop!'* over and over, and waving his arms. 'Stop this madness! Stop!' Finally, reaching the place where police and supporters were clashing most violently, he had stepped into the fray, holding aloft a white handkerchief. Once, twice, three times police batons had smashed down on his head and shoulders, before he stumbled and slumped.

That was when the commanding officer had fired the deafening shot. Snake had never before heard a gun being fired. Except in films. The explosion had been so loud he'd thought some kind of bomb had gone off. His body had begun shaking immediately, uncontrollably.

In the eerie silence that followed, the officer's voice had rung out harsh and clear. *'Everybody sit on the floor – NOW!'* They had obeyed, stumbling and knocking into each other as they tried to find space. *'Hands on heads!'* the officer had ordered. *'NOW!'*

With everybody sitting down, it had been easier to see what was going on. Two of the police had lifted Baron to his feet. There had been blood streaming from a gash on his head. Petit had jumped to his feet. 'I can help,' he had called out, his voice shaking. 'I'm a doctor.' The officer had motioned him to come forward.

As Petit had made his way out of the seated crowd, the police and the plain-clothes men had started moving in. Working their way methodically through the crowd they had forced each boy to his feet – examining faces and comparing features to the photographs they were carrying.

'This raid is part of a clamp-down on illegal UFL activities,' the officer had barked as he strode back and forth, gun in hand. 'The gentlemen in plain-clothes are recovery agents for Gunman Reds. They are looking for a runaway by the name of Easy Linker. Anyone with information will be generously rewarded.'

Closing his eyes, Snake shuddered at the memory. He had been shaking so much, the policeman had had to drag him to his feet. The helmet visor had been up. The policeman's steel eyes had peered, undecided. He had called to one of the recovery agents. The man had come over and compared the photo with Snake's face. After considering for a moment, he had waved a dismissive hand.

Only glowing embers remained of the fire. Pale grey, early morning light filtered down from holes in the roof above. But for the occasional coughs, murmurings and grunts of troubled sleep, the atrium was silent. Snake twisted his head to identify the sleeper next to him. Fluff. Her face twitched and frowned. She mumbled, her body jerked. Guessing the kind of nightmares she must be having, he placed his hand on her cheek. Her mutterings quietened, then ceased. Little by little, the frown untangled itself.

He gently stroked her head, letting his eyes wander over the other boys. Flopped under jackets and blankets, Nonce, Shiva, Grunt the goalie ... murmuring, tossing and turning, not one of them sleeping soundly. Suddenly, he froze.

The Baron, head bandaged, was there sitting in his armchair. He put a finger to his lips. 'My poor babes have had a restless night.' He sighed. 'How are you, my friend?'

'A bit shaky,' whispered Snake. 'Did the police release you?'

Baron's big head nodded slowly. 'After they'd kept me awake all night, asking questions.'

Snake coughed to clear his throat. 'What about?'

'Can't you guess ...'

Snake tried to read the Baron's expression. 'The runaway?' His voice quivered.

Baron nodded. 'For some reason, they are *desperate* to find this Easy Linker.' He snorted. 'But something tells me they won't succeed.'

Snake stared.

Baron met his gaze. Slowly a smile spread across his face. 'Just a hunch.' He winked. 'Time for this lot to smell coffee.' His voice had grown louder. Bodies were stirring. 'Wakey-wakey, my little Warriors. Rise and *shine!*'

'Baron!' '*He's back!*' Sleepers shook themselves, sat up, yawned, stretched and blinked.

'Brainstorming time,' announced Baron.

Warriors groaned.

'Brainstorming?' grunted Shiva. 'At this time in the morning?'

Baron rubbed his bandaged skull. 'Mine's not in

such good shape. But yours are young and, hopefully, should be fully functioning.' He chuckled. 'Besides which, you've all had more sleep than I.'

Snake glanced around at the dirty, sleepy faces. None of them looked particularly fresh.

'We're in a bit of a pickle,' said Baron, '– to put it mildly. As part of their petty little crackdown, the authorities are closing us down. They're going to evict us from our home.'

'They can't do that!'

'I'd like to see them try!' said Shiva. 'We can barricade ourselves in. *Defend the Castle!*'

'Our supporters would riot!'

Baron shook his head. 'Undoubtedly, God bless them. But you all saw how things were handled last night – more innocent people would be injured – and for what? In the end they'll evict us anyway.'

'We can't just surrender without a fight.'

'We are the Warriors!'

'This place is our home. Where are we going to go?'

Baron lifted weary eyes towards the crumbling walls. 'This place has been our home for some time now ...' He sighed. 'It's easy to grow attached. But sometimes being forced to move can be a blessing in disguise. This place was only ever meant to be temporary. Look at the dilapidation! Too much of our time is spent on repairs, collecting fuel and keeping out the water. This season was going to be our last.'

Heads bowed.

'The boss is right.' Shiva jumped to his feet. 'This shouldn't come as news to any of us. There's a few sites we've had our eye on for some time now. Let's check 'em out today. We can choose the best one for our new base and get on with it right away.'

Nonce nodded. 'Our next home fixture isn't for another ten days. If we get a move on, we could be out of here and into the new place, ready to play.'

Warriors murmured their assent.

'I knew I could count on you,' said Baron. 'Unfortunately, there aren't going to be any more fixtures this season. We weren't the only club to get raided last night.'

'*What!*' Warriors groaned.

'The Chief Inspector paid a visit during my interview last night.' Baron's tone was grave. 'The crack-down is London-wide.'

Gasps of disbelief.

'The whole of the London League?' said Grunt.

Baron nodded.

'Without UFL matches we're stuffed,' said Fluff. 'No matches – no money. No money – no food. No fuel.'

'Back to scavenging,' muttered Nonce.

'There have been raids and crack-downs before,' said Shiva. 'We've managed. And we can do it again. This is not the end of the world. It's not going to last for ever.'

'This *is* different though,' said Baron. 'Last night was part of something much bigger. All these stories we've been hearing on the grapevine about Todd Linker – and now they are looking for his son.' He shook his head. 'IFFA and the Affiliated Leagues have been getting jumpy for some time. They're scared about something.'

'Whenever they attack the UFL,' said Fluff, 'you know something's going down.'

Baron nodded. 'The authorities are lashing out, and unfortunately we're in the firing line. We need to lie low for a while.'

Snake looked around at the long faces. Since waking up that first time in the hospital he'd kept all thoughts about his past life pushed back, buried. He'd had to for survival's sake. He'd had to, to *be* Snake. But the raid had shaken him; the viciousness of the violence had brought thoughts of his father rushing to the surface. Where was he being held? Had he been hurt? Tortured even? Was he still alive? The thoughts had been churning all night. He had to try and find his father. 'I've got an idea …'

Eyebrows raised.

'Actually it's your idea,' said Snake. 'Dr Petit said something about how you've tried visiting a different region to play local UFL teams?' Expressions changed. He jumped to his feet. 'Why not do that *now*? If the crack-down only affects London clubs, then the regions should still be up and running.'

'Nice! But they'll have all their fixtures to play,' said Grunt. 'They're not going to have the time to give us enough games to keep going.'

Baron nodded. 'Out of season we play each team in the region and most of them several times, that's how we earn enough to pay for the trip and still show a profit.'

'But what if, instead of just limiting ourselves to one region,' said Snake, 'we keep travelling: go on a major tour, playing local UFL sides along the way. One match, then move on, sort of thing.'

'Now *that* is an interesting idea!' said Baron.

'We'd have to keep winning, of course,' said Fluff, 'or we'd run out of cash and get stuck in some tiny backwoods town in the middle of nowhere.'

'Yeah!' Tomtom sneered. 'They were practically living in the Middle Ages in the some of the places we visited.'

'And Southside's such a great place to be right now ...' Snake's sarcasm hung in the damp air.

Warriors exchanged glances.

'Maybe Snake's right,' said Nonce quietly.

Baron smiled. 'What have we got to lose?'

21

NORTH

'Round here looks as good a spot as any.' Dr Petit yelled to make his voice heard over the noisy engine. 'There's a track up ahead – I'll pull off the road. See if we can't find some cover under the trees.'

Sleepy heads stirred. Giving Fluff a gentle nudge, Snake wiped condensation from the window and peered out. Snow lay on the ground, a grey, overcast sky was dimming.

'Where are we?' grunted Fluff, leaning over him to take a look.

'A few miles from Nottingham,' sighed Snake. 'We passed a signpost a while back.' The grand tour had seemed like a good idea when he'd first suggested it, but after nearly three days cooped up in the Warriors' Battle Bus he was starting to have serious doubts.

It had taken only half a day to pack the team's belongings. They had set off straight away, reaching a hill just outside London by nightfall. Spirits had been high, the weather had held off. Eating round a camp fire, they had sung football songs and chatted excitedly about what glories might be waiting in the north.

But on the second day they'd woken to bleak skies and a cold Siberian wind. B-roads were bad enough at the best of times, but when snow started they'd been forced to slow right down. Every stretch of road had potholes, but with a covering of fresh snow they became invisible. Travel at more than a snail's pace had been impossible.

Every vehicle that used the B-roads was an improvised hybrid – cobbled together from recon-ditioned parts and cannibalized old army trucks. The Warriors' Battle Bus was no exception. Built from an ancient coach body and army transporter chassis, it could cope with more than most, but even its wheel-bearings and axles weren't up to repeated pounding from potholes.

The Battle Bus rumbled to a halt. Baron made his way along the aisle, shaking those not already awake. 'This is it. These woods are where we're pitching for the night. Tomorrow, bright and early, we'll travel into town and find ourselves some opposition.'

The crack of dawn had been a hard one. Stretching and training in thawing snow had been even tougher. Aware morale was low, Baron had given a little pep talk as they gobbled their breakfast. 'I haven't much idea what to expect from this place. It's nearly twenty years since I visited. Like most of the cities that lost their big clubs in the mergers, it's been through tough times.' He breathed warmth into his hands. 'But it's a UFL stronghold, I know that much for a fact.'

After push-starting the Battle Bus, they had rumbled their way along roads that were little more than tracks, into town. As they entered the deserted outskirts, it had looked desperate: streets of empty, abandoned houses; the occasional ragged person stopping to stare at the passing bus; the crumbling castle on its crumbling rock gazing forlornly down on the ghost of a city ...

In a side-street near the old Market Square, they disembarked. 'No wandering off on your own,' said Baron. 'Keep in pairs or small groups. I want you back at the bus by midday.' Only scant information about the cities ever reached London Town; this was unknown territory in more ways than one.

The team kitty was already low. They couldn't afford to stay in one place for too long without earning. Baron's plan was that by spreading themselves and mingling with the locals they'd have a better chance of making contact with one of the UFL sides. They needed to get something arranged quickly, so they could play the next day and move on before funds ran too low.

'This is it?' muttered Fluff, disbelievingly. 'The hub of the city?'

Under yellow-grey skies, ankle-deep in thawing snow, the crowded Market Square looked a sorry affair. Fruit and vegetable merchants displayed a meagre range of produce; other stall-holders were selling used and second-hand goods – in some cases what appeared to be nothing more than old personal belongings. The people looked thin and lacklustre, their clothes colourless and threadbare.

'I thought Southside was bad,' said Snake, 'but this ... this is *really* depressing.' They made their way towards a stall. The boy crying his wares looked about their age. Snake nodded in greeting.

'How do,' greeted the boy. 'You're not from round here.'

'We're from London.' Snake held out his hand. 'The Walworth Warriors. We're looking for a match.'

'Oh, ay?' The boy's eyes narrowed. 'Well, I can only sell you potatoes ... or onions. Try the Bell Inn ...' He turned and pointed towards a corner of the square. 'You might get lucky.'

Snake felt the boy's eyes watching as he and Fluff made their way across the square. It wasn't just the boy either, everyone was watching. It was hardly surprising, everything about them – their clothes, their hairstyles, even the way they carried themselves – stood out against the drab crowd.

'Hey, look!' Fluff pointed.

Snake turned. Slapped to the side of a tree was a poster: 'Reward For Information'. The poster looked new – a couple of days old at the most. The face in the photo was frighteningly familiar.

'Boy!' Fluff caught his eye. 'Wouldn't like to be in his boots.'

Snake nodded.

'That's one poor fool they're too keen to recover.'

The inn was crowded. Other members of the squad

were already gathered in the corner. Baron and Petit were at the bar, talking to a bearded giant. After a short time the men shook hands and Baron strode over.

'Game on!' Baron's eyes sparkled. 'That's Will Redfern, manager of the Sherwood Rangers. They're the big UFL side. He's setting up a match for tomorrow afternoon, winner-takes-the-takings. He was very enthusiastic, he's going to pull out all the stops, reckons the locals will go wild at the prospect – the most excitement they've had in a long time. Could be a massive crowd.' He rubbed his hands. 'All you have to do is *win*.'

For over a decade, Nottingham Forest's City Ground had stood empty. It had been earmarked for redevelopment following the takeover. Demolition had begun on the old Trent End stand but, with football gone from the city, local business had died and the money had dried up. Redevelopment had halted. The stadium had been boarded up.

The building had eventually been squatted and the pitch secretly maintained by a crew from local UFL clubs. On special occasions, for one-off, really big games, they opened it up. Now Sherwood Rangers' supporters had spread the word that just such an occasion was imminent. The City Ground had been readied for the match.

But the local UFL were nervous. The police, normally happy to take a bribe and turn a blind eye, had been making noises. It seemed there was a danger the game might be cancelled or cut short by a raid. Special squads of look-outs had been posted to watch for police activity; security squads had been positioned at all approaches to the ground.

The match was going ahead. The stands were filled with a capacity crowd. Where the Trent End had been partially demolished, a spectacular view opened out across the river. On the pitch with Baron and Petit, the Warriors stretched and warmed their muscles, getting a feel for the venue eleven of them were about to play in.

Baron pointed. 'That derelict building across the river is the old Meadow Lane ground. It used to be home to the other big club – Notts County.'

'The first official football club,' said Petit.

'What – the first one ever?' Snake gazed at the ruined building. 'Shouldn't there be some sort of memorial?'

Baron shrugged. 'Meadow Lane wasn't County's first home, just their last. I'm not sure anyone knows where it all started. But that sad-looking structure tells the truth of so many of the famous old clubs. We'll see more like it … if we earn enough to continue our tour.'

The crowd's chanting and singing changed into a thunderous roar, as the home team in their red-and-white kit were finally making their way on to the pitch.

Rangers' manager came hurrying over. 'Sorry about the delay,' the giant man panted. 'The game has to start right away. If we wait any longer we're going to run out of daylight – we'll be pushing it as it is.

How would it be if at half-time we simply changed ends, then carried on without a break?'

'Well ...' Baron turned anxiously to Petit. 'What d'you reckon?'

Petit shrugged. 'The boys are well rested, but ...'

'The thing is,' said Redfern, 'we'd like to avoid having to use the floodlights. We've no guarantees they work, and, even if they do, switching them on is just asking for trouble with the authorities. It's going to be touch and go as it is.'

'In that case ...' Baron nodded.

'Excellent.' Redfern shook his hand. 'Get your lads in position and we'll kick off.'

Gulping for air, Snake tried to force his lungs and heart to slow. From the kick-off there hadn't been a pause in the game, nor had there been a moment to stop and savour the thrill. The roar of the crowd had been deafening and, since there were only Rangers supporters in the stands, intimidating too. But to be playing in a proper ground was *incredible*.

When Rangers won the toss and chose ends they had known what they were doing. In the first half, the position of the sun had made little difference, but now it was low on the horizon, behind the demolished stand. Right behind the Rangers' goal.

Snake positioned the ball on the spot and squinted. The goal posts were just a thin silhouette traced against the golden glare. In the first half he and his teammates had held their own: scoring first and coming back for two more after Rangers' equalizer.

But following the quick changeover at half-time, everything had gone to pieces. Rangers had run rings round them: three goals in fifteen minutes. With only five minutes to go, they were 4–3 down. Morale was rock bottom and the sinking sun was the final nail in the coffin. In a few minutes it would be out of the way below the horizon, but by then the game would be over.

Snake paced back from the ball and waited for the referee's signal. He had to get this one. Everything depended on it. If the Warriors lost, they got nothing – that was the deal. And if they came away with no money, the whole tour was in jeopardy. *What hope then of locating his father?*

With his eyes almost squeezed shut, Snake could just make out the goalie. The crowd quietened. The referee blew his whistle. He charged, staring into the sun.

Whack …

He couldn't see a thing, but in that huge ground crowded with people, the thud of ball against wood and the rustle of netting swelled to fill the deathly hush. As the isolated cheers of his teammates died, the enormity of what he'd done hit home. He had scored *the equalizer*!

Racing back to his own half, the crowd's sullen fury pressed down on him like a rock. Every man, woman and child had smelt victory. Now they faced the prospect of going hungry.

'Everything left to play for!' yelled Baron, cheerily.

Taking their kick in a hurry, Rangers surged

forward with a new urgency, hoping to catch the Warriors unprepared. Passing on the first touch, they cut rapidly through the ranks. Their supporters, sensing salvation, leaped to their feet, screaming, cheering and shouting at the tops of their voices.

'Keep your nerve!' yelled Shiva as Warriors retreated. 'Stand your ground! Take possession!'

On the edge of the box, Fluff tackled. Hacking the ball clear, she was felled. But Nonce got to the ball and the referee signalled *Play on*. Rangers' turn on the back foot.

Finding open space, Snake ran into it. As he glanced back and yelled, the ball came curving through the air. He accelerated. Tomtom to his right, Shiva to his left. Three red-and-whites hovering to intercept. He passed right and pushed on between them.

The sun, a ball of fire, marked his target. He charged, lungs screaming. The pass came hurtling back as he entered the box. Out of the golden light the keeper appeared, sprinting, almost upon him. Snake swerved and flicked. The keeper dived.

What a thing of beauty – the ball trickling into the sunset.

22

PROGRESS

Quietly groaning with contentment, Snake rubbed his full belly and gazed out across the hall. He had never been to a banquet before. What a feast it had been! Long tables ran end to end across the large hall. Warriors, Rangers and their invited guests – family, hard-core supporters and hangers-on – had been seated interspersed with one another. Then the food had started to arrive, huge platters of roast meat and vegetables, baskets of bread, jugs of apple juice and barrels of beer. As plates emptied they were replenished. Then there had been more: home-made cakes and biscuits, cheeses, bowls of rich chocolatey pudding, baskets of fresh fruit.

Chatting, laughing and joking together, the tense rivalry of the afternoon's match had soon evaporated. Everyone had eaten and drunk their fill. Cups had been raised, toasts had been drunk and now when most of the eating had finally been done, Will Redfern, the Rangers' manager, was up on his feet, making a speech.

'Our congratulations to the Warriors on their victory ...' Opening a small satchel, to rapturous applause, Redfern held out a handful of money. 'We implore them to return again for a rematch …' The audience's laughter seemed strained, and a little uncomfortable. Redfern leant back and reached below the table. Suddenly he was holding aloft a small trophy. 'Ladies and gentlemen, lads and lasses, a big generous UFL hand for young Snake Riley – Man of the Match.'

The hall erupted: applause, cheering, shouting. People jumped up and looked around to see where Snake was seated. Nudged from his seat, he bowed his head and made his way towards the high table. The hand-clap settled into a rhythm, accompanied by table-thumping and foot-stamping. '*Snake!*' chanted the diners, '*Snake! Snake! Snake!*'

Snake scrambled up on to the platform. Will Redfern held out the silver trophy and shook his hand. '*Speech!*' chanted the diners. '*Speech! Speech! Speech!*' Their voices quietened to a hush.

The lighting was dim, but Snake could make out the faces of his teammates in the crowd. His heart felt like it was beating outside his chest. This was scarier than playing in front of thousands! He coughed to clear his throat. 'Thank you for arranging the match for us today. Rangers were excellent, tough opposition. Your hospitality and generosity have been incredible. I've never been to a banquet – *and what a banquet!*'

'*Snake! Snake! Snake!*' Again the throng chanted his name and banged the tables.

'As for this …' Snake held the trophy aloft. 'For this

I have to thank my teammates.' He touched his chest. 'To be accepted and recognized like this – you don't know what it means to me. Thank you from my heart.' The audience applauded loudly.

'There's just one last thing ...' said Snake, as the audience quietened. 'Without the UFL, today's match would never have happened. The London League has been closed down by the authorities. Who knows who's next – it could be *you*.' He raised his fist. 'Unite and fight back!'

Springing to their feet, the diners applauded heartily.

'Comrades!' Baron raised his arms for quiet. 'Comrades of the UFL ... I too would like to say a few words. As a gesture of *our* appreciation – for the way we've been so generously received, the Warriors would like the Rangers, their friends and supporters to share with them the gate from today's match.' So saying, he tipped the satchel, pouring money on to the table in front of Redfern.

The floor shook and the hall echoed with cheers.

Descending the steps at the back of the platform, Redfern gestured for Snake and Baron to follow him through the curtain.

The crowd had gone wild following Baron's money-spilling gesture. From somewhere music had started playing, acrobats, jugglers, stilt-walkers and fire-eaters had appeared, and soon everybody had been singing and dancing, jumping on the tables and joining in the carnival atmosphere.

'Those were rousing words!' Redfern clapped Snake on the back. 'Your skills are not limited to the pitch.'

Baron nodded 'Great speech!'

Redfern held out his hand to Baron. 'Thank you for your generosity, my friend.'

Baron shook his head. 'Not at all. We've seen the hardship you are all suffering here in Nottingham. Tonight's lavish banquet was a delight, but the needs of your people are no less than ours.' He nodded to Snake. 'My young star here was right – we must unite. We share a common enemy.'

Redfern glanced towards the shadows and beckoned his two guests closer. 'We had a visitor from London …' He spoke in a low voice. 'Last week recovery agents came from Gunman Reds. The police accompanied them, putting up reward posters for the boy. But before them, some time before, his father was here. He used to be a …'

'When did you see him last?' There was a quiver in Snake's voice. He glanced at Baron. 'We've heard stories about his arrest. When the police raided our club, they questioned us about him and his son. They said they were … *terrorists*.'

Baron nodded.

'I met him once before,' said Redfern. 'Several years ago. But he was here again a month or so back, travelling north. He asked about young players who had been signed by the big clubs. And, in particular, any that had been retired early or disappeared.'

'*Disappeared?*' said Snake.

'There's been a few of those.' Redfern shook his head. 'Over the years ... We gave Mr Linker as much information as we could. Of course things are pretty primitive up here communications-wise ...'

'Shhh!' Snake put a finger to his lips. With a jerk of his head, he alerted them to the shadow that had fallen across the curtain. The shadow twitched and moved hurriedly away.

Snake dashed to the curtain and snatched it open. Stepping up on to the platform, he peered in the direction in which the listener had fled. Among bobbing revellers' faces, two eyes caught his own and glanced away. *Tomtom.*

Snake woke to the sound of Baron's voice and grinding gears. The Battle Bus rolled from side to side, no doubt negotiating some particularly hazardous stretch of road.

Baron was regaling the Warriors with a re-enactment of his after-dinner speech.

Snake lifted his head. 'It was a generous act,' he interjected. 'Until tonight I'd been uncertain whether to think of you as a saint or a hard-nosed businessman.'

Warriors laughed.

'Sorry to disillusion you,' said Baron, 'but it was just a matter of good business sense. Word will get around that we're a tough side. Clubs might become wary of taking us on. But now word will also get around that we're generous. Even the most reticent will be tempted. But you can rest assured – that generous gesture won't be repeated.'

'*Top man!*' cried Tomtom.

Other voices concurred.

Baron winked, then laughed his hearty laugh.

Snake frowned.

'Who's Jordan?' Curled up on the seat next to him, Fluff glowered.

Snake twisted round to face her. 'What?'

'Girlfriend? Boyfriend? Mate? Sister? Brother? You were muttering stuff in your sleep. Sounded pretty upset.'

'He's a mate ...' Snake turned away. '... sort of. I hardly know him, actually.' He chewed his lip. 'He's an incredible player. One of the best ...'

'Did he get signed up?'

Snake nodded.

'What about you?' Fluff leant closer.

Snake glanced. Her eyes were *honest*. He nodded. 'Same club. I met him before but ... somehow we never really got a chance to play.'

Fluff leant against him. 'But you're hoping to, one day.'

23

BLADES

'The Blades?' Tomtom sneered. 'What kind of name is that for a football team?'

'There's always been a team in this town called The Blades,' said Snake. 'It used to be what the fans called Sheffield United.'

'Before they bit the dust,' muttered Fluff.

'A name with history and pedigree,' mocked Tomtom. 'Let's see what they're like on the pitch.'

Travelling up to Sheffield had taken a full day. The weather that held off for their match in Nottingham had worsened once they were back on the road and for much of the journey they'd been battling against driving sleet. First impressions on arriving in the city had been grim. It had been dark, cold, wet and windy. Exhausted and aching from the long, rough journey, in the early hours of the morning they had parked the Battle Bus in a street of derelict houses, curled up on the seats and grabbed some sleep.

This time they had an address and a contact. Although the teams of Sheffield and Nottingham were in different UFL regions, they were close enough to be in regular communication. At the crack of dawn the Warriors had been up and out – running through their stretch and warm-up routines, before Baron had them all back on the bus and heading round to the headquarters of Sheffield's most notorious UFL club.

Sheffield was even more desolate than Nottingham. Much of the town was empty and had fallen into ruin. Communities existed in pockets. Both grounds of the big old clubs had been demolished, the one to build a shopping centre – now long since abandoned – the other to make room for a cemetery, still doing very well. Though it had been Sheffield United that had originally been known as The Blades, and Hillsborough had once been home to their local rivals, it was a piece of ground beside Hillsborough cemetery that now served as home to a team called The Blades.

In the morning there had been nothing to see – just a patch of grass marked out with some rather faint white lines. There hadn't even been any goalposts. Blades' manager, Bruce Dobson, a fierce-looking man with beetling eyebrows, had agreed to the match and asked the Warriors to return after dark. They would publicize the match during the day and have the ground ready for an eight o' clock kick-off.

Dobson had talked about a flying visit to the area by recovery agents from Gunman Reds. Just as in Nottingham, they had saturated the city with their reward posters. They hadn't stayed around long – the people of Sheffield had made it clear they weren't welcome. Promising to return, they had moved off north on the fast track to Leeds.

There was no love lost for the likes of IFFA and the big clubs in UFL strongholds like Sheffield, Dobson had told them. The boy on the posters was the son of Todd Linker, Todd Linker had been their friend. There were rumours he was being held prisoner in the north-west. Dobson's assistant coach was due to return from the region shortly. Hopefully, he'd be bringing fresh news.

Pressing his face against the cold glass, Snake peered at figures shuffling along in the dark streets. Having spent the day training, practising set-pieces and then chilling out, the Warriors had set off back to the ground with low expectations. Following Dobson's mention of his father, Snake had found concentration difficult during training. Baron had pulled him up on several occasions to ask what was wrong. Unable to give the true reason, he'd blamed fitful sleep.

As the bus rolled towards the ground, Baron and the rest of the team were preoccupied with the match. With only a few hours of daylight to spread the word, how could the home team hope to bring in a crowd? How many people were going to come and watch a match on a flat piece of grass where only a couple of hundred spectators could fill the entire viewing space? In addition to which, it was cold and drizzling and had been dark for several hours.

'What the –!' Turning into the road which led to the ground, Petit swerved the bus and braked. The streets and pavements were crowded with a seething mass of people, all moving in the same direction. As he edged the bus forward, the crowd parted to make way.

'There's *thousands*!'

'Look up ahead,' said Petit. 'There's the reason.'

Where before there had been only flat grass, now two huge tiered stands rose up on either side of the pitch. As the Battle Bus rumbled slowly through the crowd, the Warriors pressed their noses against the window to stare.

'Freakin *heck*!' yelled Nonce. 'Look at the size of those stands!'

'They're massive!' said Tomtom. 'The whole population of Sheffield must be coming.'

'Looks like most of them are already here,' said Grunt. 'It's heaving with people.'

A steward in a glowing bib directed the bus on to the grass at one end of the pitch. Forewarned that the bus would have to double as their changing room, the Warriors had arrived in full kit and ready for action. They clambered out of the bus to stretch and soak up the atmosphere.

The impromptu stands had been constructed from scaffolding. Strings of bare light-bulbs twinkled around the edges like fairy lights. While stewards with torches attempted to squeeze more supporters on to benches, others were directing new arrivals into the space around the edge of the pitch. Supporters swarmed, stewards shouted orders: standing-room only at the back, benches for those who needed to sit, children on the ground at the front.

Dobson arrived to greet the Warriors. He gestured towards one of the great stands. 'As you can see, we anticipated there might be a large turnout.' He chuckled. 'And they've arrived in their droves. We seldom get visiting teams round these parts, least of all from down London way. The takings on the gate are going to be substantial tonight!'

Behind Dobson appeared two large youths. Dressed in horizontally striped kit, they carried a large sports bag between them. Around their temples, wrists and ankles there were bands of luminous blue. Their boots were illuminated by strips of the same colour. They dropped the bag at Baron's feet.

'A few extras,' said Dobson. 'Lighting's a bit of a problem with night games. These luminous strips make the whole thing a bit easier to manage. The Blades will be wearing blue luminous strips. The Warriors have got red. Our floodlights are a tad rudimentary – the illumination's not as overall as we'd like, but I'm afraid it's the best we can do.' He shrugged. 'The whole rig can be prone to failure from time to time. So when you get on the pitch you'll notice we've also got luminous lines, goalposts and ...' He bent down and reached into the bag.

'Luminous balls!' squealed Fluff.

At 5–2 down, the Warriors were getting short on patience. Squabbling had broken out before the half-time whistle blew.

'What the hell are you playing at?' Tomtom pushed Snake hard in the chest.

Fists clenched, Snake glared back. He wanted to lash out. He wanted to hit someone. Tomtom would do.

'That's enough of that!' Baron stepped between them. He glanced at Snake. 'Three goals behind! Something's going on ... let's try and sort it out. There's a lot at stake here.'

Snake met his gaze. He knew he'd been playing below par, seriously below – his concentration was shot. He knew it and his teammates knew it, but he couldn't tell them why.

Dobson's floodlights had turned out to be as unreliable as he had hinted. The game was unlike any Snake had ever played – even with the lights working at full blast, there were regions of the pitch where play was lost in darkness. The luminous strips took some getting used to and the Blades, obviously experienced in these conditions, had taken full advantage of every such moment. But that wasn't the reason for his poor performance.

Snake looked around. Sucking on their drinks, his teammates stared, each of them waiting for his explanation. Only Fluff smiled. It counted for a lot. Snake turned to Baron. 'I need a private word ...'

'OK ...' Baron gestured towards the bus. 'Let's talk.'

Tomtom glowered as Snake pushed past.

Baron puffed as he clambered up the steps behind him. 'Fire away,' he grunted, dropping into a seat.

'You're right,' said Snake, 'There *is* a lot at stake.' He sighed. 'Too much ... way too much and it's getting to me, that's why I'm messing up on the pitch.'

Baron frowned.

'I think you know who I am,' said Snake.

Baron made a low huffing sound. 'I thought I made it clear when you joined us – each player is judged on his merits, nobody has to account for his past with the Warriors.'

Snake nodded. 'But you *have* guessed?' He held Baron's gaze.

Baron's eyes flickered. He glanced out of the window, towards the team now gathered around Dr Petit. 'If you're worried someone might be tempted by the reward ...'

Snake shook his head. 'I think Fluff suspects, but not the others – they would have said.'

'What then?' Baron's face darkened. 'You're not suggesting *I* might be tempted?'

'No,' said Snake. 'I'm not.'

Baron frowned. 'Then I don't understand.'

Snake took a deep breath. 'If you've guessed who I am, then you know who my father is.'

Baron's frown deepened. He nodded.

Snake shuddered. 'Then can't you understand why my concentration's not been all it should have?'

Baron nodded. 'Those rumours Dobson mentioned, about where they might be keeping him.'

'My *father*,' said Snake. He watched Baron's face – calculating. 'I want to make a deal ...'

Baron leaned back in his seat. 'A deal?'

'I need your help ...' Snake groped for the right words. '... and the team's.'

'What are you proposing?' said Baron.

'If you help me find my father,' said Snake. 'In return, I'll continue to play for the Warriors ...'

Baron's eyebrows lifted.

'For one full season, minimum. Guaranteed.' Snake watched the brain inside the big skull calculating. 'You've never seen what I'm *really* capable of. I've been holding back, disguising my style in case someone recognizes me.'

'I'm not sure you're in a position to be making deals,' said Baron. 'There's an awful lot of money to be made just by handing you over.'

'If you were going to hand me in for the reward,' said Snake, 'you would've done it a long time ago. Maybe you just love the game too much to see a good player go. Maybe you're too smart to believe the recovery agents would really pay out. Or maybe you're just a good person ... But I'll bet you've done your calculations. You know you stand to make a lot more money out of keeping me than you could ever hope to get from any reward.'

'Easy Linker, eh?'

Snake nodded. 'That's me.' Baron was probably already dreaming of ways that the notoriety attached to the name Easy Linker might make more money. 'My identity would have to remain secret for a little while longer yet.'

'Of course,' said Baron.

There was a tap on the window. Petit beckoned. 'Three minutes.'

Baron gave the thumbs up. 'We'll be right with you.' He turned to Snake. 'One whole season, you say?'

Snake held out his hand. 'You have my word.'

'Well then ...' Baron smiled. 'We'd better see if we can find where they're keeping this father of yours.' He shook Snake's hand. 'You've got yourself a deal! Now – you've some playing to do, if you're going to make up this deficit.'

'Come on, Warriors!' Once again it was Baron's voice, backed up by Petit and the rest of the squad on the subs' bench, yelling against the roar of the massive home crowd.

The lights had been out for several minutes this time, but Snake was feeling more positive, more confident, more *at ease* than he'd felt for a long time. 5–3. With that vital first goal under his belt, he could feel something of the old flair returning. Now he and Baron had struck a deal, he had something to play for. Now the game *meant* something. But he had to be careful: the way he had taken his time over the shot – that had been pure Easy Linker, not Snake Riley. The amazed look on the faces of his teammates had said it all: this was a Snake they'd never seen before.

Running for the ball, Snake got his foot to it and twisted sharply to face the luminous green posts of Sheffield's goal. The fluorescent bands and strips made it clear which side each player was on, but in the poor light it was difficult to tell who was who.

'Snake!' Shiva's voice boomed from the penalty area.

Snake lobbed and followed.

The ball flew through the darkness towards the

goal. Luminous head-, wrist- and ankle-bands jiggled and fluttered in the dark as Blades and Warriors jumped in the goalmouth. Suddenly, with a buzz and a flicker, the lights were back on. Dazzled players flailed and collided, the goalie punched the ball clear.

Snake squinted. The glowing sphere was floating towards him. He leaped and volleyed with all his strength.

Again the keeper moved fast. This time he managed to get his body behind the ball, but the force of Snake's shot was so great that, with everyone's eyes on him, he toppled back over the line.

'Yeeeeees!' Warriors leaped and yelled. Shiva and Fluff came over to celebrate.

'Come on!' Baron bellowed from the bench. 'Two more goals in five minutes. You can do it!'

Urged on by their supporters, the Blades showed no signs of sitting back and relying on delays and defensive play to keep them their lead. Taking their kick at lightning speed, the Blades were back on the attack. But, spurred on by Snake's second goal, the Warriors threw themselves into tackling with renewed vigour.

Taking possession, Tomtom passed to Nonce, out on the wing. Shiva, Fluff and Snake pressed forward. The Blades had left a gap big enough to drive the Battle Bus through. 'Go on, Nonce!' Shiva's voice was barely audible against the crowd's noise. 'Take it all the way!'

As the Blades fell back, the Warriors charged. This time the lights stayed on. At the edge of the box,

Nonce chipped the ball across to Shiva. Shiva accelerated, jumped a tackle and tapped it sideways.

Snake made the connection. He swerved once to avoid a tackle, then again for good measure – this was *Snake* playing. He was right in front of the goal and travelling at speed, but the goalie was hunkered down and waiting. Snake leaned to the left and dummied a strike, lifting the ball across for Fluff. Fluff dived, heading the ball with maximum impact. In spite of the glow, the goalie never saw it coming.

'Five all!' Baron's triumphant roar cut through the groans of the disappointed Blades supporters.

There were just a few minutes on the clock. Now both sides had the prize in their sights. Taking the kick with their accustomed speed, the Blades threw all their players forward. Only the keeper remained in defence. With short passes and fast runs they moved the ball forward to the roar of the crowd. The Warriors kept their heads, marking and blocking. But little by little the Blades edged their way to the box.

From the eighteen-yard line, The Blades' blond striker took a power-shot at goal. Grunt, the Warriors' goalie, punched it clear, but the danger wasn't over. Blades swooped. Warriors blocked, hacked, and blocked again. Players were toppling left, right and centre, but the ball was still in play as Snake ran into the breach.

A Blade was turning to shoot. Flinging himself feet-first, Snake slid along the slippery turf and clipped the ball clear. Fluff was there to take possession. She trapped it, twisted free of a tackle and raced towards open ground.

In a flash, Snake was up on his feet and running. So, it seemed, was every other player on the pitch. The crowd's roar swelled. Fluff was fast, but she wasn't the fastest on the pitch and she knew it. As she ran she cut left, glancing from side to side, in anticipation of support from her teammates.

Snake accelerated like a rocket, pushing past one player after another, over the centre line and into Blades territory. He was up with the chasing pack and inching ahead. Shiva was level and Fluff over to his left. Two Blades were on her heels. The crowd bayed for blood. Snake forced his legs to go faster. *'Fluff!'*

The Blades made their move. Fluff went down, chopped at the ankles, but she flicked the ball free. Stretching to reach it, Snake felt a tug at his collar. He twisted and jerked, but the choking grip persisted and the ref was looking the wrong way. Snake slashed at the offending arm, flailed, broke free and took possession. Now Shiva and Nonce were ahead. There were Blades everywhere, running helter-skelter, back to defend. Lofting the ball to the wing, he broke free.

With Blades trying to cut him off, Nonce stretched his long legs to out-flank them. The referee checked his watch as he ran. Sensing imminent danger, the crowd began to whistle in anticipation of the final whistle.

'Come on, Warriors!' Baron's deep voice boomed through the din. 'There's still time for that winner!'

Hurtling towards the corner post, Nonce swivelled

at the last minute and hoofed the ball high. It soared. Shiva, Tomtom and four Blades were charging ahead of Snake towards the goal. Tomtom jumped, two Blades followed suit. Shiva was next, stretching into the dark sky. The ball jerked from his contact, flying wide. Snake lunged, whipping his left foot high to hook the ball back where it belonged.

The whistle blew. And then again. Two short blasts.

24

LIAISON

'At last,' said the man. 'The famous Warriors! Your reputation precedes you.' He offered his hand. 'Terry Gunther – boss of *Gunther's Haulage*, and managing-coach at Shaddongate.' His jumper was inscribed with the words 'Shaddongate Football Club'. Hand-knitted, it looked old and baggy.

Baron introduced himself and shook hands.

Petit and Snake followed suit.

The grapevine had worked its peculiar magic. When Dobson's assistant had arrived back in Sheffield on a *Gunther's Haulage* truck, he had not only brought them word of Todd Linker, but a connection to him. And now, after three days on the B-roads, the man Dobson's assistant had told them about, a man who had seen Todd Linker with his very own eyes, was standing in front of them.

Gunther's eyes flickered anxiously. 'I understand you're interested in a certain party?'

Baron nodded. 'A friendly Sheffield acquaintance led us to believe you might be able to help.'

'Please – ' Gunther gestured towards a door

marked 'Office'. 'This is something we should discuss in private.' He nodded towards the bus. 'If your squad want to collect their stuff off the bus, a couple of my lads will show them to where they'll be staying.'

While Snake followed Baron and Gunther into the room, Petit returned to the bus to help supervise. This was the first time they'd been offered accommodation by a club. The Warriors were going to be delighted – it would certainly make a change from camping and sleeping on the bus.

Gunther closed the door and turned to face them. 'I'm sorry. We have to be very careful. UFL's enemies have their spies.' He indicated for them to sit. Making his way behind the desk, he sat facing them in the large swivel chair. 'Todd Linker is being held, courtesy of IFFA and Gunman Reds, at HMP Lancaster Castle.'

His Majesty's Prison. Snake shivered. Images of his father in cramped dingy cells had flashed through his head so many times over the past weeks. He had tried to dismiss them, to blot them out with other possibilities. But now here was confirmation. It was true: his father was a prisoner.

'This part of the country actually has one of the oldest footballing traditions,' said Gunther. 'But Lancaster itself has never been much of a football town. As far as I know, it's never had its own club. Of course there have always been amateur sides in the area, but none has ever linked up with the UFL. That, in my opinion, is why they chose the place.'

Baron frowned. 'That makes things very awkward.

We can't just roll into town looking for a match like we've done before. Is there no football at all?'

'What there is is strictly amateur – local farmers, traders, and youth sides.' Gunther's eyes twinkled. 'But I think I have a way we might get a few of your squad inside the castle gates.'

Snake squirmed in his seat. 'Let's hear it!'

'Are either of you, perchance, familiar with the story of the Trojan Horse?'

Snake and Baron exchanged puzzled glances. They nodded.

'Excellent!' Gunther's face grew animated. 'I have a sister who lives in Lancaster. My niece and nephew are football mad. Both play for Codmins YFC, a local youth side. I know the team well – occasionally, I go over to assist with the coaching and help out.' The eyes twinkled more brightly. 'Because there aren't many teams about, Codmins get to play regular friendlies against HMP Lancaster Castle FC, a mixed team of inmates and warders from the prison. In three days' time, they've got their next match inside the prison.'

'How does it work?' asked Baron.

'There's a simple routine,' said Gunther. 'Whether the game is home or away, a prison vehicle is always used for transporting players in and out through the gates. Codmins YFC are delivered in the prison's small bus. The vehicle brings the squad, the coach and whoever else in through the gates, straight to the sports and recreation building.'

'The game's played indoors?' said Snake.

Gunther shook his head. 'No, that's just for the showers and changing facilities. Matches are always played in the prison yard. They cancel if the weather's diabolical.'

'Who gets to watch?' said Baron. 'Any of the inmates?'

'Yep.' Gunther nodded. 'All of them who aren't playing, from what I can make out. It's only a small prison. That's how come I saw Todd Linker.'

'You recognized him?' said Snake.

Gunther nodded again. 'He visited Carlisle a while back. One of our old boys used to be a scout for him when he was still running things at Gunman Reds. Linker made friends a-plenty round these parts. He was up here trying to gather evidence about the big clubs and their antics.' Leaning forward across his desk, he glanced from one to the other. 'I take it you know something about his little investigations?'

Baron and Snake nodded.

Gunther's eyes narrowed. 'I don't care if it's legal or otherwise. It's a desperate state of affairs when young boys are being fed cocktails of drugs as a matter of course.' He shook his head gravely. 'I don't call that sport.'

'Todd Linker was trying to get something done about it,' said Snake. 'That's why they locked him up.'

Gunther sneered. 'And once again Gunman Reds are champions of the British Premier League.'

Snake felt a sudden surge of pride. *But his team was now his enemy*. The feeling turned sour. He frowned. 'That's official?'

Gunther nodded. 'They play Kölner Krieger in the Charity Shield.' He sighed. 'But people are tired of the way things are. They're hungry for change.'

'Among those we've met on our travels,' said Baron, 'Todd Linker has been a lot more popular than Gunman Reds.'

'Or any of the other big clubs, for that matter.' Snake felt his heart pound. 'If we could free him ...'

Gunther nodded. 'The man has more than enough allies to start a *revolution*.'

25

PRISON

The small coach crawled its way up the hill. Now that the gates of Lancaster Castle Prison loomed ahead, a week's worth of planning and rehearsing seemed of little comfort. Clutching himself to stop the shivers, Snake glanced at the faces: Baron, Gunther, Petit, the Codmins' coach and the hand-picked men Gunther had brought down from Carlisle to accompany them as 'parents'.

Fluff, Shiva and Nonce looked transformed: piercings removed, tattoos covered over with make-up, hair cut to look as normal as possible – pictures of innocence, all dressed in their Codmins trackies. The rest of the players were a mixture of the real thing, including Gunther's nephew, and those Shaddongate boys whom Gunther had chosen. All sat, hunched in their seats, chatting with nervous excitement as they would before any match.

The big gates swung open. The coach gave a shudder, before lurching under the stone arch and through into a bleak courtyard. A uniformed guard directed them towards the far corner. Parking in front of a single-storey building, the driver cut the engine. 'Here you go.' He chuckled. 'May the best team win!'

Like all the prison buildings inside the complex, the windows were enclosed behind metal bars. While the four Warriors and the rest of the Shaddongate squad busied themselves stripping down to their kit and putting on their boots, Baron and the men went over to the windows to familiarize themselves with the prison layout.

As Snake bent to tie his boots, he felt a hand stroke the soft stubble on his scalp.

'Suits you, captain!' Fluff grinned. Without her nose and eyebrow rings her face looked less severe. 'Who you playing as today then?' She winked. 'Snake? Or the other one?'

Snake felt himself blush. How long had she known? He smiled. 'I think Snake's playing days might be over.'

There was a knock at the door. 'The prison team are coming out into the yard,' barked a fierce voice. 'They're ready whenever you are.'

'Right.' Baron beckoned for everyone to gather round. 'We all know what we have to do.' Heads nodded. 'Remember to wait for the signal.'

It was the strangest feeling, playing in the knowledge that, if all went according to plan, the end of the game would never be reached. Goals mattered, but keeping the guards entertained and drawing them into the match mattered most. The prison team had extra height and power, but the Codmins had the speed and flexibility of youth. Both sides could have benefited from more team-practice and training.

Snake had felt panic when they'd first walked out. As he'd scanned the players and spectators, he'd been unable to spot his father. If he wasn't there, *how were they going to rescue him*?

Coming up behind, Fluff had nudged him out of his frozen state. 'Don't worry,' she'd whispered. 'The warders aren't going to miss this game, it's the only entertainment they get. Let's make it a cracker. They'll bring him.'

Sure enough, twenty minutes into the first half, as the home team celebrated their second goal, two guards emerged. Snake had to force himself not to stare. His father looked thin and haggard, but, as the trio joined the other prisoners and guards on the sidelines, he raised his head and surveyed the pitch. Snake felt his father's stare flicker over him. *Had Dad recognized him?* The next time Snake risked a glance, Todd Linker's expression was as lifeless as before, but he had straightened his back.

'Come on, Codmins!' The coach cupped his hands round his mouth and bellowed. 'We've got a game to win!'

Suddenly, Snake felt a surge of energy. The game was going according to plan. Dad was finally there where they could all see him. The signal would come when Baron decided everything was right and ready. Till then there was a job to be done. He sprinted at the burly forward as he made a bee-line for the Codmins' goal.

The prison team all looked the same in their blue-and-white kit with their short-cropped hair. Who was inmate and who warder? It was impossible to tell, but this one had scored the first goal and looked determined to notch another. Dropping his weight low, Snake stabbed the ball free and chased after it. Behind him the burly forward cursed.

Arms shot in the air from Nonce on the right wing and Fluff in midfield. On the left Billy, the Codmins' winger, had thrown off his marker and found himself a good, clear path. Recalling the form the boy had shown in training, Snake took aim and lofted the ball. It soared, a perfect diagonal arc. Billy raced to meet it, turning in towards the centre as he trapped it. 'Man on!' yelled Shiva. But Billy had already seen the threat and, before the defender could trouble him, the ball was back in the air floating towards Fluff in the centre of the box. Perfect.

'Go on, girl! yelled Petit and the crew.

'Put it past 'em!' bellowed Baron.

Defenders stumbled and collided as Fluff swerved first one way then the other. The prison goalie crouched and glared.

'Shoot!' yelled Codmins' coach. But Fluff kept on going. At the last minute the keeper lost his nerve and charged out to meet her. Cool as a cucumber, Fluff skipped to the left and tapped it past him. It rolled ... in off the right post.

'*Yeeeeees!*' As the Codmins celebrated, furious home defenders berated one another for the lapse. There was no mistaking their body language – frustration and outrage. Beaten by a girl! To add insult to injury, Fluff skipped daintily back to her teammates.

Snake embraced her. 'Perfect!' he whispered. 'Now stay out of their way, they'll want to kill you after that.' Glancing over to the sidelines, he caught Baron's discreet nod. There it was – *the signal*. 'OK, Codmins!' yelled Snake. 'Let's show this bunch of losers.'

'That's right!' bellowed Baron. 'Let's show them!'

'*Game on!*' roared the team in unison.

Taking their kick, the prison team edged forward more cautiously than before. The Codmins and their supporters goaded and heckled. 'What's their problem?' 'Can't take being beaten by a few boys and a girl?' 'Look at them – quaking in their boots.' 'Can't face the shame of being thrashed by a bunch of kids?'

Scowling, the blue-and-whites pushed forward. But their edginess showed in inaccurate passing. They shouted at one another and cursed as they struggled to regain or maintain possession. Codmins harried and fell back, waiting for Snake to make his move. With a long, straight pass, the burly forward whom Snake had tackled earlier sent the ball soaring to the wing. Snake charged.

The massive, mean-looking winger was right on the sideline, still trying to control the ball as Snake came up beside him. 'Come on, tough guy!' hissed Snake effeminately. 'Let's see you get past me.'

The winger's face darkened.

'Come on, you big soft streak!' Snake winked. 'Are you doing something with that ball, or what?'

Nostrils flaring, fists clenched, the winger lunged –

straight at Snake. There was no pretence of going round, with his sheer size he wanted to mow him down and trample him underfoot. But Snake side-stepped, toe-poked the ball and gasped, feigning injury. As the giant winger stumbled past, Snake crashed back into him, full force from the side, elbows into ribs. The winger grunted and flailed, Snake ducked, shrieked in pretend agony and grabbed the winger's sleeve. Together they spun, careening straight into the gaggle of onlookers.

Cries of 'Foul!' and 'Ref!' went up from all around. Behind them more shouting and yelling broke out as other players from both sides ran to join the fray. Throwing his arms round the winger's neck, Snake clung to his back as he lurched and crashed into guards and inmates.

In twos and threes the Codmins players steamed into the crowd, jumping on guards, pulling them to the ground and disarming them. Seeing the opportunity to settle old scores, the shackled prisoners were quick to turn on their jailers. In no time at all a huge mêlée of blue-and-whites, uniformed guards and prisoners, Codmins and their hand-picked 'parents' was spilling across the yard. The referee's whistle blew again and again. Now it was joined by other whistles blowing and a siren's wail as the guards tried to summon reinforcements.

Snake had jumped off the big winger as the man finally went crashing to the ground, tripped by one of the Codmins boys. Now, dodging wild punches and grappling bodies, he pushed through the fray. Some of the guards had simply given up and run for it when they'd seen how badly things were going. But the two guarding his father were struggling to drag him back towards the building. '*Warriors!*' yelled Snake. 'To the rescue!'

The guards turned, batons drawn.

'Yaaaaaaaaaaaagh!' Screaming with all the fury he could muster, Snake charged. One guard pushed Todd Linker back against the wall, the other stepped forward, wielding his baton double-handed like a club. Snake ducked and sprang, launching himself, shoulder first, at the man's stomach. The guard gasped and doubled over. Snake staggered on across the concrete.

Snarling like a beast, the second guard slashed with his baton. Snake threw himself to the ground, rolled and scrambled to his feet. Over to his left, Nonce, Fluff and Shiva came running. 'The doc's secured the gate,' panted Fluff. Nonce nodded. 'Baron's bringing round the coach.'

Behind them Shiva clutched a bloodied nose. The first guard, still on the ground, groaned and stretched in a vain attempt to reach his baton. Kicking it out of reach, Shiva stamped on his wrist. The guard yelped.

The eyes of the second guard flitted from his fallen colleague to the Warriors. As they fanned out around him, he growled, shaking his baton at each of them in turn. Across the yard the coach horn sounded over the shouts and skirmishing. Snake stepped forward. 'Our fight isn't with you,' he said. He stared straight into the guard's eyes. 'Let my father go.'

'Your father?' Nonce and Shiva turned and stared.

The guard's eyes narrowed as he bared his teeth and raised his baton to strike. Behind him handcuffs glinted. Todd Linker's fists came down hard. The guard's head shook, his knees buckled and he fell to the ground.

'Nothing personal ...' Todd Linker stepped over the body. '... but some of us have a bus to catch.'

26

DARK FOREST

The father-and-son reunion had been all too brief.
As the prison bus tore out through the gates, he'd resigned himself to being 'Easy' once again. Too many knew to keep it secret.

The rough and bumpy escape-route had been meticulously planned, there were traps and obstacles to halt would-be pursuers, and hiding places to watch the road behind. Petit's skilful driving did the rest.

Along the way, Easy had recounted his adventures to his father, starting from the moment he and Trix had returned home on his birthday. He had lowered his voice when he'd got to the part about the micro-disc and Munro Sweet. Todd had leant close and listened keenly. By the time they arrived at the rendezvous, the decision had been made – the two of them must separate immediately. Father and son captured together would be fatal to their cause.

At a derelict farm, vehicles and teammates had been waiting as prearranged. Abandoning the prison bus, the break-out team had split into three groups for the next part of the journey. Easy had travelled by the worst of B-roads with a full complement of Warriors in the Battle Bus. His dad had gone with the Codmins crew, who had taken their ancient cargo transporter via a more direct route. Terry Gunther and the Shaddongate crew had headed for the site a third way.

The gathering under the trees would be an unforgettable experience. Lookouts had been posted at intervals around the meeting-place. The need for secrecy dictated that they meet in the heart of the forest and, to minimize the chance of detection, lamps and candles were being kept to a minimum. It was hard to gauge the numbers.

Accompanying his father as he mingled and greeted, Easy was introduced to visitors from far and wide – from towns across Scotland, the north of England and the Midlands. Some had even travelled up from the south and southern Wales. Each was a personal acquaintance of Todd Linker's, each a link to a disaffected region or excluded community.

Todd had prearranged the forest meeting-place on his travels. During the week that the prison break-out had been planned and rehearsed, Gunther's drivers had delivered a coded message across the country. Contrary to what he'd led the Warriors to believe, he and Todd were old friends from the days when he'd been Todd's talent-scout for the north-west. They'd been preparing for this gathering of the disaffected when Todd had been nabbed on the road from Glasgow.

As Todd Linker stepped up on to the giant tree-stump, Easy found himself a space near by at the edge of the clearing. The gathering quietened in anticipation.

'First of all, let me thank those of you who rescued me from incarceration.' Todd bowed his head. Mutters of 'Here, here!' rippled through the gathering. Todd raised his head again, his eyes scanning the shadowy faces. 'Without your brave efforts our great project might have died before it could be born.'

Easy felt a hand squeeze his arm. He turned to see Fluff grinning beside him. Other Warriors were sitting or standing close by.

'An historic opportunity stands before us ...' Todd's eyes glinted in the flickering light. 'All of us here know at first hand the devastation that has been inflicted on our communities. A consequence of greed, a consequence of policies that have fostered that greed, a consequence of corruption.'

The gathering murmured and nodded. Todd Linker surveyed the faces. 'All of us here have been touched by the harm that this greed and corruption have caused. And in particular, all of us know only too well the particular effect this has had on the sport that is not only our national passion, but our communal life-blood.'

For a moment the gathering seemed to forget themselves as they applauded and cheered with abandon. But Todd's raised hands soon reminded them of their dangerous circumstances. They quietened.

'Friends ... for too long we have seen our communities ravaged and the quality of our lives decimated.

We have watched helplessly, as the almighty corporations have wreaked their havoc on our nation, poisoning the institutions that lie at the very heart of our society and our way of life.'

'That's right!' shouted an angry voice.

'What kind of nation,' continued Todd, 'what kind of world do we want to live in? One in which the dispossessed masses are milked dry by a super-rich privileged few?'

Murmurs of 'No! *No way!*' filled the dark clearing.

'It's time for change.'

'*Change!*' echoed the gathering.

'If we act together now, we can bring about that change.'

'*Now!*' echoed the gathering.

'At the weekend, a delegation from IFFA will be arriving in Britain. On a whistle-stop tour of the major stadiums in preparation for the World Cup, they'll visit Manchester, Newcastle and Glasgow. They'll also, of course, check out the London venues, before finally being whisked over to the giant new People's Stadium at Wembley for the International Charity Shield.' Todd paused for the gathering to assimilate the information. 'That doesn't give us much time.

'We've already heard stories about road-blocks. The authorities are very keen to recapture me, for obvious reasons. However, they are probably even more desperate to get hold of my son, for reasons which I'll let him explain.' Todd turned and beckoned to Easy.

Easy clambered on to the tree-stump and stood beside his father. 'With the help of my friend Jordan ...' His voice croaked from nerves and emotion. '... I gained access to a computer in a high-security medical building while training at Gunman Reds. The computer contained classified medical files on all Gunman's players including those who have been "retired" and those forced out of the game through sickness and injury.'

Easy glanced at Fluff. She smiled reassuringly. 'Among other things,' he continued, 'the files listed all the enhancers and other drugs which are and have been given to the players. I managed to copy them on to a hi-sec micro-disc.'

The gathering cheered.

Easy shook his head. 'It's not that simple. I don't know if anyone's familiar with these discs ...?'

Heads shook.

'What about them?' asked Fluff.

'When you copy stuff on to them,' said Easy, 'both disc and computer store voice-pattern and iris-pattern fingerprints for security. The computer keeps an ID record of the person doing the copying.'

Faces looked puzzled.

'So that's why they've been searching for you,' grunted Tomtom. 'Because they know you've stolen their files?'

Easy nodded. 'The micro-discs are high security, they can't be duplicated or printed. The only way to make another copy of that information would be to copy it from the screen.'

'Which, under the circumstances,' said Todd, 'there wasn't the opportunity for Easy to do.'

'Things were a little tricky,' muttered Easy.

'In practice,' said Todd, 'this means there's just one copy of our most valuable piece of evidence.'

'But to make things more complicated,' said Easy, 'that data can only be accessed by the person who's voice and iris fingerprints match those on the disc.'

'And that's Easy,' said Todd.

Easy nodded.

Todd draped an arm across his son's shoulders. 'So we have to look after him!'

There was laughter from the gathering.

'When I was arrested,' said Todd, 'much of the evidence I had gathered was confiscated. I had managed to conceal duplicates of some of that evidence, and I know a few of you were able to do the same with material you passed on to me. But the fact is – this micro-disc, to which my son is our only link, represents by the far the most damning piece of evidence we could hope to possess.'

Heads nodded. There were murmurs of agreement.

'As many of you have already discovered on your journeys here,' said Todd, 'the authorities wasted no time setting up road-blocks. They're making no bones about who they're after – Todd and Easy Linker. The rewards they are offering are high, my friends, the penalties for harbouring either of us – *severe*.'

Todd pointed away through the trees. 'By now there'll be road-blocks on every road entering London. Our enemies are not stupid. They know that if our evidence should get out during this delegation's visit, it could finally blow the lid on their evil machinations ...' Todd's finger jabbed the air accusingly. 'IFFA, the government, the pharmaceuticals, the big clubs, we're going to expose *the whole corrupt lot of them.*'

With hushed murmurs, the gathering raised their fists towards the night sky.

Glancing at his father, Easy did the same. 'Fair play!' he cried.

'Fair play!' echoed the dark forest.

27

LONDON

The streets looked very different during the daytime. They were narrower and much more crowded than before. But of course they couldn't be narrower – that was a trick of the light. And as far as being more crowded went, well – people came out in the daytime, didn't they? And London was positively bustling with extra people in advance of the big Charity Shield contest. There seemed to be police patrols on every street corner, in vehicles, on motorbikes, on foot; they were stopping people, questioning them and occasionally even making arrests.

'You're certain it was Southside?'

Easy nodded. He was sure this was the right area. His head had been spinning horribly that night, he'd been so ill ... but he remembered seeing the signs as the cab had taken him over the river. 'There was this church near by. A football church. Amazing place, what was it called ... the Sacred Oracular ...'

The Warriors were staring at him like he was off his rocker. 'A *football* church?' said Nonce.

'Who's ever heard of such a thing!' wheezed Tomtom.

Shiva shook his head. 'No football church round here, mate.'

'No, listen –' Easy scowled. They didn't believe him. 'There was this huge neon sign ... the words spelt out "SOCCER". What was it? The Sacred Oracular Church of Christ's Eternal Redemption, or something. Inside there were these amazing stained-glass windows of Pele and ...'

The entire bus was laughing at him. *Was it really that ridiculous?* He slumped back into his seat.

'Don't take it personally.' Fluff punched him on the arm. 'No one's having a go at you. It's a great idea.'

'But everyone thinks I'm making it up.'

'Not making it up,' said Fluff. 'It's just we all know this area like the back of our hands and there is no football church here.'

'Or anywhere else as far as I know.' Baron sat down in the seat opposite. 'It's not so improbable though, in this crazy world. I expect it's something your imagination came up with.'

'I imagined it?'

'Hallucinated – you were in the early stages of withdrawal from all those chemicals Gunman Reds had been putting into you, remember? That can do alarming things to the brain.'

'But if I, or my brain, made it up ...' Easy felt an awful sinking feeling. 'Maybe the rest of it's not true either. All this driving around – we could be wasting our time. Maybe there is no basement bar.' Doubt filled his mind. 'Maybe there wasn't even a micro-disc.'

'Oi!' Fluff tapped him on the arm. 'What's this then?' She pulled up his sleeve.

The snake tattoo.

'You told me you had it done in the basement bar. You said it was about the last thing you could remember.'

'Subterrania!' yelled Petit from the driver's seat. 'Here we go – basement bar on the corner. Ring any bells?'

Jumping to his feet, Easy hurried down the aisle. 'That's the one! *That's it!*'

Fluff slurped noisily, sucking the remains of her milkshake up through the straw. Grabbing a stool, Easy sat beside her.

Fluff slid a second milkshake over in front of him. 'Did you find it?'

Easy pushed the milkshake back. 'It wasn't there.'

'*What!*?' Fluff jerked round. 'What d'you mean? Are you *sure*?'

Easy nodded. 'Positive. I searched several times. It's gone.' He stared at the poster behind the bar. *Gunman Reds versus Kölner Krieger. International Charity Shield*. And scrawled underneath by hand: *Tomorrow night – LIVE!*

'It can't have gone.' Fluff slid from her stool. 'Let me ...'

'Whoa!' Easy grabbed her jacket, pulling her back. 'I checked *thoroughly*. OK?' He glanced round. It was that feeling of being watched. A couple of boys playing table-football laughed and continued with their game. A girl in the corner pushed her dark glasses to the bridge of her nose and reached for her drink. He was probably just being jumpy. Memories from the last time he was here?

Fluff scowled.

Easy nodded towards the second milkshake. 'Keep slurping. We're not supposed to be drawing attention to ourselves, remember?'

Fluff obeyed. 'What are we going to do, now?'

'I don't know,' said Easy. 'Rack our brains?' They were on their own. Baron and Petit had intended to come in with them, but the youth on the door had turned them away, pointing to a sign: *No admittance to anyone over 21 or under 12.* They were back in the bus with the Warriors, parked up the street on the lookout for cops. Or whoever.

'You could try asking the barman,' suggested Fluff.

'What – Excuse me, I left a package on top of the cistern in the gents, has anyone handed it in?' It was Easy's turn to scowl. 'I don't think so.' He shivered. The feeling of being watched was still there. He glanced in the mirror behind the bar. The girl in the dark glasses appeared to be staring. She rose to her feet. Tall. Black leather trousers. Black leather waistcoat. Tattooed arms. She walked towards him.

'Snake?'

Easy felt Fluff stiffen beside him. He turned.

The girl frowned and pushed the dark glasses up into her hair.

Pierced lip. Keloid scars on the cheeks.

'It *is* you, isn't it?' The girl reached out and pulled up his sleeve. 'Ahhh!' She smiled. 'I thought so – one of my masterpieces! Boy! You've changed.' She stroked his head. 'Amazing what a bit of hair and eyebrows can do!'

The tattoo girl!

Fluff swivelled on the stool and dug him in the ribs. 'Aren't you going to introduce me to your friend?'

'Who's this?' The smile stretched wider. 'Your girlfriend?'

Easy felt Fluff clutch his arm and press close. He blushed. 'We're uh … teammates.'

The girl glanced from one to the other, eyes narrowed. 'Oh, really?' She held out a hand to Fluff. 'Selina. Pleased to meet you.'

Fluff introduced herself.

'So, to what do we owe the pleasure?'

'My boyfriend left a little package in the toilet,' said Fluff. 'He came back to collect it, but it's gone.'

Still blushing, Easy met Selina's gaze.

She lifted an eyebrow. 'You're a dark horse, aren't you. I never took you for the hacker type.'

'Hacker?' Easy frowned.

'Computers – you know.' Selina frowned back. 'That's what it was, wasn't it? A computer disc?'

Easy nodded. *She knew!*

'Have you got it?' said Fluff.

Selina nodded. 'Not me. My boyfriend – back at the flat.' She laughed. 'On top of that cistern's where he keeps his stash!'

'Stash?' said Easy.

'Yeah.' Selina nodded towards the poster behind the bar. 'Tickets for the big match. He touts.'

Selina's boyfriend grinned and folded the bundle of money into his trouser pocket. 'Pleasure doing business with you, dude. A *pleasure!*'

Baron tucked the tickets inside his jacket.

'Now ...' The boyfriend held out his palm to Easy. 'Dude!'

Easy slapped.

'I thought you must be a secret agent or something. That's a Hi-Sec micro 5000 you got there.' The boyfriend grinned a toothy grin. 'But I guess you know that.' He beckoned. 'Come through to my lair.'

Easy followed him into the next room. Banks of monitors, computers of various shapes and sizes were stacked on boxes, shelves and a desk.

'It's a hobby.' The boyfriend cleared papers off a chair. 'Make yourself comfortable.'

Easy sat.

The boyfriend clicked a mouse. A monitor to his left flickered into life. 'Here ...' He handed over to Easy. 'You'd better do it.' Ducking under the desk, he fiddled with some wires. 'OK. Go ahead. Camera and mike's connected.'

Easy clicked on the icon for the micro-disc. The familiar screen message appeared: *'Hi-Sec micro 5000. Iris and voice scan. Please state your name.'*

'Ajax Morayne.'

The boyfriend chuckled. 'Cool!'

The machine whirred. The screen flickered.

'Bingo!'

Selina and Fluff came hurrying into the room.

'What's happened?'

'Have you done it?'

Baron peered over their heads. 'Are the files there? Is the information there?'

Easy nodded and scrolled the names.

'Wow!' The boyfriend pointed at the screen, his voice an awed whisper. 'Ajax Morayne's file!'

'They're all here,' said Easy. The scrolling stopped. He clicked on the file labelled 'Jordan Snapes'. The screen refilled … 'Someone grab a pen and paper.' He gazed at lists: dates, names of drugs, quantities administered, effects observed – just like the ones he'd seen before.

Sitting beside him, Fluff began to copy them down.

'Right,' said Easy, 'time to get in touch with our MP.' He clicked on the email icon and a small window appeared in the bottom half of the screen. *Meet tonight*, he typed. *Snake Riley*. He turned to Baron. 'What's our new address?'

'One Wharf Lane,' said Baron. 'Rotherhithe.'

Easy's fingers clattered on the keyboard. Done.

The vast old riverside warehouse smelt musty, it felt cold and damp – but that was something they'd been used to. The roof had a few small holes, but that was something they could fix. It was an enormous space, probably not as large a full-size pitch but not far off. The ceiling was high and it was easily big enough for the UFL's requirements.

While Dr Petit worked on connecting up the electric power for the lights, the Warriors and the newly arrived Shaddongate squad worked by torch-light under Baron's direction: a few of them unloading equipment from the Battle Bus, the rest making a start on clearing away the piles of old empty crates and rubbish. The previous tenants of their new headquarters had not left it tidy. There would be plenty to burn for the next few weeks.

Easy and his father sat huddled by the huge doors, taking it in turns to watch the dark cobbled street and exchanging stories about their difficult journeys south: the obstacles they'd had to get round and the police patrols they'd had to outwit.

Headlight beams sliced the darkness. From the top of the street a long, dark shape rolled towards the warehouse.

'Someone's coming!' hissed Easy.

Todd's short, sharp whistle echoed in the vastness. Behind them the chatter, the activity and the torches flickered and died; the warehouse became silent and still. Easy peered through the crack between the giant doors. Bouncing softly along the cobbles, a swish limousine pulled up to the kerb.

'Take a look,' whispered Easy.

Todd put his eyes to the crack. 'No one following. Looks promising ... can't be many people drive around in one of those.'

Easy felt a nudge.

'Give us a hand with this door.'

As the crack widened, Easy put his weight against

the door's edge. Reluctantly it rumbled along the runners. In the street, the rear door of the limousine opened.

Easy switched on his torch and shone the beam at the figure emerging from the car.

'Snake Riley, I presume?' Hand outstretched, Munro Sweet walked towards him through the night.

28

WEMBLEY

The streets of Wembley were a sea of people. Easy had never seen anything like it in his life. A mass of red and white. Everyone, it seemed, had come to see the nation's champions play.

Swamped by vehicles pouring into the capital on every B-road, according to rumours: police road-blocks had finally adopted a policy of turning back all but those carrying proof of urgent business and those with tickets for the big match. But they had acted too late. Todd's network of contacts had done its work and all around the country people had been converging on the capital in their thousands. On many roads, overwhelmed by sheer numbers, police had been forced to abandon their road-blocks and beat a hasty retreat.

Over the last two days, giant screens had been erected in parks around the capital in an attempt to draw the ticket-less hordes away from the giant stadium. But the authorities' efforts appeared to have had little effect. Though the police were out in force on the streets of Wembley, they had seemed nervous in their riot gear, as if sensing that their numbers were but a drop in the ocean of chanting, excited citizenry.

Nevertheless, now that the Warriors had finally reached the turnstiles, Easy's heart was beating so loud he could hear it above the crowd's excited chant. *We're going to Wem-ber-ley! We're going to Wem-ber-leeee!* The walls of the stadium were peppered with wanted posters of him and his father.

Behind the turnstiles, riot police waited with dogs. The man inside the ticket booth peered at Easy then pushed open the door behind him and spoke to someone out of sight. Seconds ticked by; frustrated voices called out from the queue behind. Easy felt his knees begin to shake. Then the man was back. The turnstile clicked and Easy pushed through towards his teammates and the wall of police. But before he could breathe a sigh of relief, a figure stepped out from beside the booth and placed a firm hand against his chest.

'I'd like to take a look at that ticket, young man.'

Easy froze and handed his ticket to the towering man in uniform.

'Everything all right, officer?' Baron's big face beamed, then grimaced as he struggled to squeeze through the turnstile.

The policeman's moustache twitched. 'Just routine – spot checks. There's a lot of forgeries about, you know.' He nodded to Easy. 'This your boy?'

'Well ...'

'He's my son, officer.' Todd Linker's red-and-white-striped face appeared over Baron's shoulder.

The policeman smiled. 'Ah! I can see the resemblance.' Pointing at Easy's painted face, he laughed. 'Like father, like son!' He waved them through. 'Enjoy the match!'

The last few weeks and months had provided more than their fair share of stress and tension but, as far as Easy was concerned, the few short minutes it had taken him to enter the stadium had topped the lot. His nerves were jangled. Yet now he was here in the great stadium – with his father beside him and teammates on either side, tiers and tiers above, more tiers below and all around – he felt light-headed, almost giddy.

'A penny for them …' Todd Linker dropped a bag of warm doughnuts into his son's lap.

'I was just thinking: *Phew!*' Easy chose a doughnut and bit. It tasted marvellous. 'And: *Now what?*'

'Now we just have to sit and wait.' Todd Linker smiled. 'And let old Munro work his magic.'

Down on the pitch, a line of three men in suits walked out from the central stand in dignified procession. As they grouped in the centre of the pitch, their faces appeared on the big screens. All of them were faces Easy recognized; one was Munro Sweet.

'Ladies and gentlemen …' The PA boomed, the crowd rustled in their seats and grew silent. '… boys and girls, *everybody* – welcome!'

The crowd applauded, whistled and cheered.

Todd Linker leant towards Easy. 'Emmanuel Garcia,' he yelled. 'President of IFFA.'

Easy nodded.

'Welcome to this, the People's Stadium of Wembley. Welcome to the International Charity Shield!'

Again the crowd sounded their approval.

The smile filled the big screen. 'We are honoured to have with us today the UK Minister for Sport. Allow me to introduce Mr Michael Marley.' On the pitch the figure of the IFFA president could be seen handing over the microphone to the second man in a suit.

The more sombre face of the Minister for Sport now filled the giant screen. 'As you are all no doubt aware, the authorities have unfortunately been forced to delay today's kick-off.'

The crowd greeted this comment with groans and whistles. This wasn't news – the kick-off had been due some forty minutes ago.

'This delay has primarily been due to the severe crowding of the local area and the need to allow extra time for ticket-holders to get to their seats.'

Easy glanced at his dad. Todd Linker held up crossed fingers.

'However, there has also been a rather unusual development with several unforeseen circum-stances ...'

The crowd grew silent.

The Minister for Sport cleared his throat. 'Over the last twenty-four hours several documents have been brought to my notice by member of the opposition, Mr Munro Sweet, MP. The information contained in these documents is of a very serious nature and pertains to the way in which football is currently being conducted in this country.'

Easy felt his father's hand squeeze his shoulder.

'Because of the complex nature of this information I do not propose to go further into the matter at this juncture. However, tomorrow the government will be announcing a full public enquiry into the state of football in this country. That enquiry will include a thorough investigation into every aspect of every major club with a base in this country, both BPL and Corporates League. That is our promise.'

The Minister for Sport turned to the President of IFFA and spoke away from the microphone. The President nodded and spoke back. 'I understand from the President,' said the Minister for Sport, 'that tomorrow IFFA will also be announcing a similar public enquiry on an international level into all clubs competing under their auspices.'

Pausing for the crowd to absorb what had been said, the Minister for Sport glanced nervously towards Munro Sweet. 'I would now like to hand over the microphone to the member of the opposition.'

The familiar face filled the big screen, neither smiling nor frowning. 'It is probably no exaggeration to say that everybody here in the stadium today *loves* the game of football.' Sweet slowly turned, taking in the huge mass of people gathered around him.

Cheers and whistles echoed. Easy glanced around, others were doing the same.

'We,' said Sweet, 'are the privileged few. For every one of us in here there are many thousands out there ...' He pointed. '... who love the game just as intensely. Football is in the blood of this nation.'

The crowd roared its agreement.

'But over the course of the last few years ...' Sweet's voice rose up, silencing the crowd. '... that blood has been *poisoned*!' On the big screen his face was stony. 'International corporations have transformed our national football heritage for their profit, corrupting government and sports bodies along the way and turning young men and boys, the cream of our footballing stock, into little more than drugged puppets.'

It was as if the whole stadium, all two hundred and fifty thousand of them, had held their breath.

Sweet solemnly nodded his head. 'That's what our beautiful game has come to.' He gestured towards the Minister for Sport. 'You heard the promise made by the Minster just now – it's up to all of us to make sure that he and the government keep that promise.'

The crowd murmured their agreement.

'Fair play!' Sweet raised his fist.

'*Fair play!*' echoed the crowd.

'Fair play!' yelled Sweet, 'not just in football, but in all things, and for *all*!'

'*Fair play!*' chanted the crowd. '*Fair play! Fair play! Fair play!*'

Sweet's fist punched the air in time to the crowd's chant. He smiled as the chant became a deafening roar that filled the stadium. Finally holding his hands aloft for silence.

'Because of the serious nature of the evidence my good friends have collected, in addition to the measures the Minster has announced, the government has also, at long last, decided to impose compulsory blood-testing of all competing players. To take effect as from *now*.'

Easy glanced at his father as the crowd roared its approval. Todd Linker smiled and shrugged. 'This,' he yelled, 'is better than I'd hoped!'

'However ...' Again Sweet held his hands aloft to be heard. '... this decision has unfortunately resulted in a rather awkward situation.'

The crowd fell deathly silent.

'Kölner Krieger, champions of the Bundesleague and runners-up in this year's European Cup, were to have been the opponents for Gunman Reds in this International Charity Shield match. But they have, at the last minute, made a decision of their own ... I am sorry to have to announce that they will no longer be playing.'

The crowd erupted, booing, jeering and cheering.

'Even better!' Todd Linker clasped his hands. 'IFFA will be forced to follow suit with the blood tests!'

'However ...' Once again Sweet raised his hands. Once again the crowd fell silent. 'There is a team here in the stadium who I'd like to invite to take their place.'

The crowd muttered excitedly in expectation.

'This team,' said Sweet, 'has acted with the greatest courage to help bring about these changes we see beginning here today. They don't play for the BPL ... they don't play for the Corporates League ...'

The crowd went silent.

'This team, my friends, is a UFL team.'

Easy felt his stomach churn. The crowd had erupted again, but this time it was split between groans and gasps, boos and cheers. He turned to Fluff.

Fluff's fierce face cracked into a smile. 'Are you thinking what I'm thinking?'

Easy nodded.

On the big screen Sweet smiled and pointed up into the stands. The picture leaped to a different camera. The new image focused high up in the stands. A row of faces, some smiling, some ashen. 'A big People's Stadium welcome for the Walworth Warriors!'

Easy felt a tug at his sleeve. The crowd roared. Mesmerized by his image on the giant screen, he rose to his feet.

29

FAIR PLAY

Something about it all felt strangely familiar, even though he knew he'd never been in the People's Stadium before. He couldn't have, this was the first time anyone had ever changed in the dressing rooms. And in a minute it would be the first time teams had walked down the tunnel and played on the pitch.

Flanked by the two linesmen, the referee stood waiting at the entrance to the tunnel. Easy couldn't help staring, there was something about his face and manner that was so familiar. But where from? He had seen the man before, he *knew* he had, but not in a referee's strip.

Catching Easy's glance, the referee smiled. 'Ready?' Two rows of perfect teeth gleamed whiter-than-white against ebony skin.

Easy turned to check his teammates. Some were shaking their arms and legs to keep the muscles warm, others stretched. Everyone was busy doing something to keep their minds off the enormity of what they were about to do, to keep from *panicking*. At the back, Baron, Petit and the subs chewed gum impatiently.

Easy nodded to the referee. 'We're ready.'

The opposition's dressing-room door opened and, with the clatter of studs, Gunman Reds jogged out and formed themselves into a line beside the Warriors.

Recognizing the face at the front of the line, Easy felt his knees go loose.

Ajax Morayne grinned. 'You still have traces of red and white round the edges of your hair.' Wiping Easy's forehead with his thumb, he showed him the proof. 'You a Reds fan?'

Easy nodded. 'The biggest!' Ajax Morayne looked massive. So did the rest of the team.

'OK?' The referee raised his eyebrows and tapped his watch. Morayne nodded.

'At last!' The referee clapped his hands together. Let's do it.' With his linesmen he turned and set off down the tunnel. Behind them the two teams followed. The narrow space filled with the echo of clattering studs.

At the head of his team, Easy fought to control his nerves. A mixture of excitement and terror was making him shake, his teeth were chattering. Playing in the ultimate stadium in front of a capacity crowd – it was what he'd always dreamed of.

'*Gunman Reds! Gunman Reds! Gunman Reds! Reds! Reds!*'

But in his dreams, there was one small difference. He was always playing on that other side, the team the entire stadium was shouting for.

As the two teams ran out on to the pitch the crowd erupted into a deafening roar. Easy jogged his way to the centre alongside the referee and Ajax Morayne.

'A big welcome for our referee here this afternoon ...' The loudspeakers boomed. '... Reverend Shankly Obeah.' On the big screen, the Reverend nodded in acknowledgement of the crowd's applause.

Easy stared at the man in front of him.

'I think we may have met before.' The Reverend referee winked and produced a coin from his pocket. 'Who's calling?'

Ajax Morayne gestured towards Easy. The referee flipped the coin.

Easy shook himself. 'Heads!' he yelled.

'Heads it is!' Placing the ball on the spot, the referee turned and walked away.

'*Gun-man – Gunman Reds! Gun-man – Gunman Reds!*' The chanting resumed again in earnest.

Ajax Morayne began to pace back from the ball. 'So tell me,' he called, 'my little Gunman supporter ...' His eyes narrowed. '... what do you think are your chances?'

'Fifty–fifty.' Easy stood tall. 'What are your chances of passing the blood test?'

Morayne scowled. The whistle blew. Easy passed back to Fluff.

The atmosphere in the dressing room had been mournful. Baron's words of encouragement had made little impact on the dejected team. Forty-five minutes of fighting a rear-guard action, with the crowd baying for Gunman goals had sapped them all.

In spite of Baron's insistence that they'd brought off a miracle to be only two goals down – the team's faces had shown they weren't convinced.

Easy raised his hand. 'Can I say something?'

Baron nodded.

'Our tactics have been the right ones,' said Easy. 'Right from the start we agreed we had to save our attack for the last quarter. The two goals against us are nothing to be ashamed of.'

He rose to his feet. 'We have to keep our heads … we have to keep our nerve. We've fought a lot of tough battles recently, but to win this last one we have to *believe*.' Picking up a ball from the bench, he clutched it to his chest. 'Each of us has to find the strength in our hearts and the will to do it.'

It had felt like the strangest moment ever – as he'd left the changing room, Dad had pulled him to one side and nodded towards three figures a little way up the corridor. Mum, Trix and Deena.

He had hurried over. Mum had kissed him, Deena and Trix had hugged him. Trix had whispered, 'Dad says: if you get the chance to score an early goal, take it!' Deena had whispered, 'I'm sorry.'

There had been no time to think or speak. He had simply hugged them and hurried to catch up with his teammates.

When he'd walked out of the tunnel, he'd felt different. He'd felt proud. He had felt in control. He had walked tall. And ten minutes into the second half he had scored the early goal.

The crowd had been stunned into silence. Gunman Reds had brought on substitutes and thrown everything they'd got at them. The Warriors had kept their heads and their nerve. Then their advances had begun to be greeted by cheers from the stands.

But now there wasn't time to think about such things. The crowd were working themselves into a frenzy. Both teams were playing with everything they had, the good moves of each side – the passes, the tackles, the runs – received increasingly rapturous cheers and applause. Baron had just made the signal. It was finally time to ratchet up the game.

'Tomtom!' Easy charged into open space, hand raised.

Glancing up, Tomtom lofted the ball, clean across the heads of half a dozen players.

Easy caught it on the run. Nonce was on the far right, Fluff, bobbing and weaving, was hurtling up the middle. As Easy accelerated, the crowd let out a roar of anticipation.

Gunman defenders frantically yelled at one another to fill the gaps.

Easy churned past one. He skinned a second, just yards from the box. His legs were screaming. 'Fluff!' he yelled, chipping the ball as a tackle came in from the left. The crowd leaped to its feet and went frantic.

Instinctively Easy thundered on, chasing the action. Fluff dodged a tackle and passed wide to Nonce. With a single perfect touch Nonce passed it back. Gunman's goalie came charging out, arms stretched.

'Keep your head!' yelled Easy. And Fluff did. Running straight at the keeper, she waited for his dive. With the gentlest of taps she poked the ball through his legs, skipping over his prone body to tap it into the net.

If the stadium had had a roof, it would have lifted. The force of the sound felt like it was shaking the foundations. The Warriors mobbed Fluff in celebration, before jogging back to their own half.

Easy watched their exhausted, elated faces. They had made all the substitutions they were allowed. Did they have what was needed for one last push?

The loudspeaker system boomed with the announcement of Gunman Reds' final substitution. 'Jordan Snapes for Ajax Morayne.' Easy stopped dead in his tracks. And stared.

As the crowd applauded, Gunman's double goal-scorer clapped his hands above his head and walked to the bench. On the sidelines he slapped palms with the substitute. Jordan sprinted towards the centre. Halting by the ball, he looked across at Easy. 'You've been busy!' He grinned. 'Good to see you, my friend. At last you get to show me what you're made of.'

Easy felt a surge of elation. The weariness, the aches and the pains simply vanished. He grinned. 'At last!'

The whistle blew.

Jordan passed inside and charged forward. The player passed straight back. Easy closed for the tackle, but Jordan shoved him off and accelerated into the Warriors' half. The Gunman forwards tried in vain to keep pace with their substitute, the Warriors harried and went in for the tackle. But Jordan seemed invincible – jumping, swerving, dodging one way then the other, he weaved his way towards the Warriors' goal.

Easy gave chase. This was ... *personal*. He charged, driving his legs faster and faster, gaining on Jordan as he continued his unbelievable run.

Defenders converged to block. Jordan cut right. Flinging himself across the turf, Easy clipped the ball away from the nimble feet and went sliding after it. As he scrambled up he glimpsed Jordan thundering towards him. He spun, threw himself sideways and took off at a run.

The crowd whistled and shrieked.

Easy scanned the field and passed, straight out to Nonce.

'Come on!' Jordan flew past him, yelling at his teammates as he gave chase.

Nonce didn't know what hit him. Within seconds, Jordan had crossed half the width of the pitch and recovered the ball. Now the crowd were urging him on.

Yelling to his defenders. Easy raced like a demon to intercept. He was filled with a furious energy – as if Jordan might somehow single-handedly destroy all they had worked for. Charging blindly, he closed down the gap and homed in for the tackle. This time there was no sliding, just the deftest tap and a skip. Then he was running, running for all he was worth. With Jordan and half the Gunman Reds chasing back after him.

And now the fickle crowd were with him, roaring in his ears, as he twisted round one player, jumped the tackle of another, pushed past a third. The roaring grew louder. Pitch and players became a blur. He forced his legs faster and faster. Only one thing remained clear, and he hurtled towards it like there was nothing that could stop him.

He sensed Jordan keeping pace with him somewhere to his right, just edging ahead, trying to cut across in front. Easy's lungs were on fire. He could hear Jordan's gasps. He wanted to laugh. It was only a game! Just a few seconds more. He was about to explode. One last lunge and ...

'GOOOOOOOOAL!'

The People's Stadium of Wembley erupted.

As Easy clutched the post, panting for breath, two blasts on the referee's whistle sealed the result, and the crowd doubled its roar. He felt a hand on his shoulder.

'Brilliant goal!' gasped Jordan. 'I have to admit – you are the best,' he grinned and panted, *'for the time being.'* There was a moment's pause. 'But when they give me the OK to play again ... I want a rematch.'

'No problem!'

'Easy! Easy! Easy!'

Easy turned to acknowledge the roaring crowd.

Suddenly the sound changed. Laughter and whistling swelled inside the cheers and applause. Easy jerked round.

Jordan grinned. But for his boots and socks, he stood *naked*. 'I never forget a bet!' he chuckled. Behind him, Fluff, Shiva and the other Warriors clutched themselves, laughing.

'I'm really sorry ...' Easy covered his mouth to hide his smirk. '– you asked me to pray that when we finally got to play it was somewhere discreet ...'

'You forgot?' said Jordan.

Easy shrugged.

'Capacity crowd.' Jordan gestured towards the stands. 'Two hundred and fifty thousand!'

Easy smirked. 'Plus another hundred million watching worldwide.' Jordan laughed and blushed. 'I was worrying all that time on the bench!'

'Come on!' Easy slapped him on the back. 'You have to join us for the lap of honour!'